With Louis and the Duke

THE AUTOBIOGRAPHY OF A JAZZ CLARINETIST

With Louis and the Duke

THE AUTOBIOGRAPHY OF A JAZZ CLARINETIST

by

BARNEY BIGARD

Edited by Barry Martyn

MACMILLAN PRESS
Music Division

First published 1985

First published in paperback 1987

Published by
THE MACMILLAN PRESS LTD
Houndmills, Basingstoke, Hampshire RG21 2XS
and London
Companies and representatives
throughout the world

Printed in Hong Kong

Typeset by Rowland Phototypesetting Ltd
Bury St Edmunds, Suffolk
in 11/12pt Caledonia

British Library Cataloguing in Publication Data
Bigard, Barney
    With Louis and the Duke.
1. Bigard, Barney   2. Jazz musicians—
United States—Biography
I. Title   II. Martyn, Barry
788'.62'0924   ML419.B5

ISBN 0-333-40210-3

The editor and publisher gratefully acknowledge permission to
reproduce photographs from the collections of the following: Ray
Avery, Dorothe Bigard and Floyd Levin. We are extremely grateful
also to Duncan Shiedt whose photograph appears on the front cover.
    Every effort has been made to trace all the copyright holders, but if
any have been inadvertently overlooked the publisher will be pleased
to make the necessary arrangements at the first opportunity.

Contents

Editor's Preface

Barney Bigard and I first crossed paths in Montreal in 1961. He had just
finished a concert at the Forum with the Louis Armstrong All Stars and
I had gone backstage, to shake hands with the band members. Barney
was immediately conspicuous by his absence. "He's over there in the
wings fixing his clarinet," said Trummy Young. Of all the people in the
band besides Louis, Barney was the one I wanted to talk to most of all
because he was from New Orleans. When I was a couple of feet away I
said, "Mr Bigard. I know your brother Alex from New Orleans." He
stared blankly at me and replied, "So?" After a few bland pleasantries,
all one way, I bid him goodnight and we picked up the "conversation"
again nine years later in Los Angeles. My band from England was there
to play the *Hello Louis!* concert for Armstrong's 70th birthday at the
Shrine Auditorium. I wanted to introduce my clarinetist to Barney and
again we found him in the wings after the show. "Mr Bigard. We met in
Montreal some years ago. My clarinet player wanted to meet you," was
the opener. "Right! Good to see you both again," was the closer. It was
clearly "case dismissed" and that seemed to be the end of the line as far
as verbal contact went with the jazz giant.

A week or so later I went to dinner with the instigator of the *Hello
Louis!* show, Floyd Levin, and his wife Lucille. They called that same
afternoon to tell me that Barney and his wife Dottie were to join us. I
remember thinking to myself, "I hope his wife talks more than he
does." Over the next ten years I learned that this was not a man to waste
words in any shape or form. He and his wife became my closest friends
in the country. It took a while, but over the years he became like a
second father to me. I could not begin to tell of the feeling I held for
him. It's enough to say that I was his friend, and, even more important,
he was mine.

I don't know precisely where or when the idea for this book came to me. It must have been in 1972 sometime. "Barney. Why don't you write a book?"

"On what?"

"You."

"Oh I don't have time for that."

"Well," I said, "since we get together to chew the fat anyway, we just need to bring a tape recorder and that's that." Here, thirteen years later, is the result of that work.

Barney must have been the all-time hardest interviewee. For one thing, he was not the world's best talker, seconded by the fact that he was the most modest man I have ever met in the jazz world. But as the weeks went by I began amassing a solid pile of tapes. I tried to keep all of them in some kind of sequence; some of them had the same stories twice but all were important. He told his tale the way he saw it, spun silver-webbed accounts of the early days in New Orleans, solid gold stories from many an era long gone, and it all started to come into place. The hardest thing was to get him to say anything about his own contribution to it all, but as time passed I began to realize that this was not so important. The very fact that he was with all of these people spoke for itself. They were all telling his story for him.

Almost two years of afternoon interviews went by and finally Barney said, "Well, I guess the book is about finished." The "fun" part was over. It took the next seven years to get the book ready to go to a publisher. It could not have been done without the help of a jazz fan named Cody Morgan who transcribed the tapes.

When the work was over and done, the tapes were donated to the Institute of Jazz Studies at Rutgers University, New Jersey. There they will remain for all time.

Barney left on 27 June 1980 . . .

Barry Martyn
New Orleans
May 1985

Introduction

It was in Chicago that I first met the man. He was working across the street from me at the Plantation with King Oliver. I used to love to go over and hear Joe's band, especially when he would tell the guys, "I want to hear the shuffle of the people's feet." That was his expression and the band would play just that softly.

Barney was playing mostly saxophone then and we would hang out at the Union to shoot pool and talk. In fact, that's just where I first got to meet Louis, right in that Union hall. At that time I was with Jimmie Noone at the Apex Club, but I always liked Barney's style that much more. He was more advanced on the clarinet. I mean the things he was playing: all those arrangements and stuff was much more difficult than someone just playing around on the side with small groups.

When I was at the Grand Terrace one night I saw a picture of Duke's band and there was Barney. That's how I learned that he went with the band. It's so easy to pick him out on the records they made. His style is so distinctive. He was always on the driving side, but like an elephant, sure-footed. He wasn't the guy to miss notes and try to cover. He knew what to play and he played it.

As far as tone: you know, it's a funny thing about all those New Orleans guys. That's one thing they dwell on: the tone. Open, you know, not piercing.

In the forties I had a club in Chicago and I had heard Louis was forming a small six-piece outfit to play Billy Berg's club in Los Angeles. A couple of weeks later I had a phone call from Joe Glaser asking me to join them, replacing Dick Cary. I joined them at the Roxy Theater, then went to Europe for the Nice Festival.

I was glad to be with them. I mean, Barney, Big Sid, Jack and Louis. Oh, each of them was a star in his own right. That much I knew, although I didn't know some of their numbers, like *Muskrat Ramble* and *Panama*. But I soon got them down.

At Nice we really got together, musically. It was my first trip. Barney had been there years before with Duke, but he played differently with our All Stars group. His feature numbers were *Tea for Two* and *I Surrender, Dear*. I always cared more for background and harmony in a band than solos, and he was just great to play behind. Inspired, you understand. In fact, I used to get mad with him in the band because he would only take one chorus. I used to love to hear him play. That's the only trouble we had with him, except for those soft-shell crabs: Barney is just crazy about soft-shell crabs.

Nowadays we only play together at festivals and big shows. We did play the Hollywood Bowl some years back, and last year the Timex Show out of New York. We see each other when we can.

I just wish the musicians today had the same attitude towards the profession as we had then. No animosity, always passing ideas. In truth, if any of these youngsters today would talk with Barney for just two minutes, they would realize that here is a guy that came up through the ranks. He hasn't picked up on things just overnight. He knows his music, both reading it and playing it with ideas and feeling. In other words, a true professional.

I am glad I could write the introduction to this book. We are friends and have been for getting on for half a century. In quiet moments I will enjoy reading how he did it all. It will be a real, simple pleasure to me.

Earl "Fatha" Hines
January 1974

PART ONE

ONE

"All my people, they all spoke French."

New Orleans was one hell of a town. Then, now, anytime. There is something about the place that grabs you. It's such a mixture, a melting pot of peoples and races: artists, sailors, writers, whores, poets, pimps, and just about every kind of person you can think of. It's like a "gathering place for lost souls." People came there from all over the world, some out of choice, some by force and some because, like me, they simply happened to be born there.

I arrived in New Orleans on 3 March 1906, born to two people known as "Creoles of color," which was essentially a mixture of Spanish and French. Like I said, there was such a mixture down there that the birth of one baby boy wouldn't seem to affect the total tally to any extent.

My mother's name was Emanuella and she died giving birth to me. My father, Alexander, stayed grieved for a while and then remarried, after leaving me with the tag of Albany Leon Bigard to tote through this life. My grandmother raised me and I called her "mom." This pleased her and she repaid me by shortening my name to "Bon-nie." It was a step in the right direction at least. Over the years it became closer to Barney, for which I shall be eternally grateful.

My grandmother's name was Eugenia. She was French Creole and Spanish and had long hair almost to her heels. She was a lovely woman but she could hardly speak any English at all. She would speak it all backwards, any kind of way. But she was a wonderful woman— beautiful too.

I spent my early years with my grandmother and my grandfather, Jules, at 1726 North Villere Street in the city of New Orleans. My grandfather was about to become sexton of the graveyard. You see at that time they wouldn't put bodies in the ground because New Orleans is below water level and there was constant seepage and floods from Lake Pontchartrain and the Mississippi River. They put them in vaults above ground. They were fixing one, preparing it, and a sack of cement dropped and some went in my grandfather's eye. They didn't think of using warm water. They used cold water and so he was blind for the rest of his life. We had a doctor that the whole family used to go to twice a week so that he could cut some stuff from around the pupil, hoping that it would get better. It never did.

From then on he couldn't work, but he was phenomenal. He used to get up in the morning and light a fire in the stove, make the coffee, saw wood. All that kind of business. He'd go all through the house with no help at all. He knew that house backwards. Even though he was completely blind he owned a couple of extra houses so he got along. He didn't need no help. We were not rich, but we wasn't poor in other words. In fact the family could make a dollar go a long way in those days. For instance, there was a thing that the grocer had called "quartee." This meant half a nickel; like you could buy a quartee of red beans and a quartee of rice and feed your whole family. They would get a piece of salt pork for practically nothing and stick it in there and that was a dinner. Sometimes they would make "Gumbo Zerbe." This was a conglomeration of different vegetable leaves such as cabbage leaves, mustard, and all that stuff with salt pork added to make a whole big dish. They knew how to manage and we got along like that. We never did want for anything because my uncles used to help out a lot.

One of my uncles was named Ulysses and he had a cigar factory. It was no big place but it was right in back of our house. He had about six guys in there working for him. Another uncle, Emile, was a professional musician—a violinist in fact—so my earliest recollections of the world outside the home were cigars and music. Both were to play a part in my youth.

When my mother died my father moved away for a while, but then when he remarried he moved into a house about a block away from us and carried on with his insurance business. I was lucky in a way because before my mother died she and my father had had two other children —boys—and so I had brothers. The oldest one was named Alex after my father, and then came Sidney, then me. I always wanted a sister but couldn't have one. Pops missed the boat.

My oldest brother, Alex, was born about five years before me and we were never very close because he wanted to be a man before his time. In later years he took up music and became a drummer. He lived and died in New Orleans. My other brother, Sidney, was about my size and he and I were the only ones that had any togetherness because we went to school together. As he grew up he became more of a loner until he was killed in an accident. He used to drive a six-mule team. He never was a musician. He was a hard-working boy.

I was about five or six years old when I first started to go to school: the Marigny school. I'll never forget that. I attended Straight University for about two years but then I got tired. While I was at Marigny I used to draw a lot on the blackboard, especially around Christmas and Thanksgiving. I would draw a turkey or Santa Claus or reindeer. Things like that. Everybody kept encouraging me to take it up, but I couldn't see it.

When we were young all of us neighborhood kids would play rough, but that didn't last long because we got interested in doing things to pick up money. We would collect old bits of brass or take tin foil from the cigarettes and make it into a ball. The bigger the ball, the more money we would get. We did pretty good. We also used to get some soft red brick and pound it into a powder. The women in our section would scrub steps, or stoops as they called 'em in New Orleans. And they'd put this red brick dust with yellow ochre and make those stoops come out beautiful. We got a nickel a bucket for the brick dust and you could get into a theater for that, so we'd pound, pound, pound, all day long.

On Saturdays we used to play ball in the street and we would hear a parade coming. That's really my first interest in music: as a kid watching the brass bands. We'd hear the parade coming down the street and, well, that was the end of that game. We would try to follow the band as far as our folks would let us. That would generally only be for four blocks or so. They didn't want us to get hung up in those "second lines" because they were kind of bad.

We kids were able to tell which bands were which too. Some bands would have like blue denim shirts and white pants, and another band would have white shirts and red pants. In any case, the grand marshall would always be up in front and most times behind him would be a banner with the band's name, like "Tuxedo Brass Band" or something. I remember a lot of times they didn't have the same men each time. A guy might be a bass violin player but if he got hired for a brass band job he would go get some kind of bass horn. He would move to get the money.

After a while we kids began to take more of an interest in bands. I remember at that time they would often park a wagon on our street corner to advertise for a ball. What they had was a furniture mover's long truck with a horse or mule drawing it and they'd get the band in that wagon. They would all be seated with the trombone on the end with the bass so they could hang out a bit. Well, they'd advertise a ball for that same night. That's why the wagon would come out, and they'd stand on a corner where they thought a lot of people would be and play a couple of tunes.

Bands like Kid Ory's and Papa Celestin's were very popular about then. One might be giving a ball uptown and the other might have one downtown and they would be out in the streets advertising and they would meet up at one corner or another and have a "battle" to see who was going to "cut" the other. If one was getting cut real bad the people would chain the wagon wheels together. The winner was decided by the people and that's the ball they would go to that night. The people would clap their hands and dance in the street right there on the corner. Whichever band had the nastiest lyrics would win. Like Ory had a tune to which the band sang "If you don't like the way I play, then kiss my funky ass." This went over big with all the whores and they would gather around the wagon. Another real foul-mouthed man was Frankie Dusen who played trombone.

Us kids would stand and watch all this going on and it was a whole lot of fun. In fact, where I began to appreciate music was right there in the streets. I had an idea I wanted to play trumpet but the family they had a funny idea that it would take too much wind to play the trumpet so they said "If you want to play something, play clarinet." I could whistle pretty good so I guess they thought that I would make a clarinetist some day.

Meanwhile I had started to work in my uncle Ulysses' cigar factory, in back of our house. I started out sifting tobacco on the floor. I'd get the dust out of the tobacco and he gave me 50 cents a week. This was pretty good because I was only about twelve at the time. Soon I started rolling bunches, and then I began rolling tobacco so good next thing you knew I was a cigar maker.

When I began making cigars the factory got $8 a thousand but if you got to be good at it you'd go on to a better cigar. The price would go up the better you got until you reached the pure Havana cigars. They got $50 a thousand for them. But they had to be made just so. You were not even supposed to see where the wrapper turns around, and the head, it'd better be just perfect. Then there was what they called "pin tails" with the small end that had to be perfectly put together, otherwise they couldn't pass it.

I never was very fond of my uncle Ulysses because my grandmother had told me that one Sunday when I was a baby the family was all having dinner and I was brought to the table crying like mad. And my uncle Ulysses he said, "Why don't you take that kid and give it a spanking and make him stop all that damn noise?" Grandma said "No! There's something wrong with this baby. Nobody's going to spank this baby." She got up from the table and started looking me over and found a diaper pin that was sticking into me. Then she raised up my arms and I had boils under both of them. She called my uncle and said, "Look. You wanted to spank this kid. Look." So after that he felt like shit. She told me that in later years. If I had have known it when I was young I never would have gone to work for him.

Anyway, when I was about fourteen I used to stay away from the factory so I could go to the Lyric Theater to see stuff like Ma Rainey with Joe Smith. I was becoming more interested in music than cigars by now, especially since my uncle Emile was a musician, and also I talked with a clarinet player that worked for my other uncle's cigar factory by the name of Luis Tio. So after three or four years I got tired of making cigars, the way they would keep the factory all closed up with no ventilation. On top of this all the cigar makers smoked all day and I was getting sick, so I just gave it up. I didn't want no more of it. I figured that I would get to know my other uncle, Emile, and music just a little bit better from then on.

TWO

"I wanted to be a musician."

Most of my family were on my father's side. My mother's family name was "Marquez" but most of her people were killed in a hurricane. They were fisherman people that lived by Lake Pontchartrain until one day a hurricane blew up and around twelve or thirteen of them were blown into the lake. There was just one survivor. They never even found the bodies of the rest.

Like I said, most of my family was on my father's side and as a young boy it seemed to me that the whole bunch lived at our house. I mean, besides Alex, Sidney and me there was my grandmother, my grandfather until he died, then my father's sister, and Uncle Emile. He was my father's half brother. You see my grandfather married twice.

Anyway, Uncle Emile used to go to work as a musician but in the daytime he would be at home practicing a whole lot. I used to listen to him playing from that method book he had. His teacher was A. J. Piron and after he had learned the violin from Piron he went out on his own. When I was young, though, I would hear him playing his exercises from his method book or sometimes he would be teaching himself the straight leads of different songs. I never did care for the violin so much but I loved it when he rehearsed the band he was with. He called a rehearsal and they would all come to the house. Uncle Emile was the leader of a band called "Kid Ory's Creole Ragtime Band."

Ory's band was a soft playing band at that time. They had Mutt Carey (trumpet), Johnny Dodds (clarinet), Kid Ory (trombone), Wilhelmina Bart (piano), George "Pops" Foster (bass) and Henry Zeno (drums). They played nice and soft which was just what the people wanted to hear at that time. Like schottisches, waltzes and even some Scott Joplin pieces. You see what made my uncle leader was that most of the guys in the band couldn't read worth beans. A couple of them could "spell" a little and so when a new tune would come out usually the violinist, who had more musical knowledge than most of the others, would go and buy the sheet music and call a rehearsal. The violin would play the straight lead for them and keep on until the trumpet player got it. When the trumpet had it down then the rest of them would fall in with their parts. A lot of people talk about those early "New Orleans" bands, or "Dixieland" bands, but they all forget that most of the bands had a violinist as the leader. Those early bands didn't sound anything like the kind of jazz bands that you hear today. Nothing at all.

I know for a fact that Ory could never read, and Johnny Dodds couldn't either. He wasn't a Creole but came from uptown, and, to tell the truth, when I heard him he never did impress me much. The guys in the band were always talking about a clarinet player named Lorenzo Tio, who I knew was the nephew of the old man I had worked with in the cigar factory. It was a long time though before I heard him play in person.

I used to listen to Ory's band rehearsing at the house for years before I really showed an active interest in music. I wonder that those characters ever allowed me near them after I had been so bad in my earlier years to them. When I was much smaller I used to run in and pull all their music down just for devilment. They would take a break and there I would come and down would come all their stuff. They would run me out of the house every time.

But of course, as time passed, I wanted to be a musician. It grew on me, I imagine. Then I listened more seriously to what their band would do. For years I had nurtured the idea to play trumpet, after seeing and hearing all the music around me, but finally the family got together with me and told me that if I learned the notes and such first then it wouldn't be so hard for me to learn an instrument. They asked Uncle Emile to help me and he sent away for a book of music to Sears Roebuck. I'll never forget the name of that book. It was called *Lazarus Music Book*. When we got it he began to teach me the names of the notes—F.A.C.E. and so forth—then how to divide them. Finally they figured that I should start with a real instrument and so instead of the trumpet my father bought me a second-hand E flat clarinet. So that was my first instrument, the E flat clarinet. I don't have the faintest idea of what it cost, it was probably a Conn or something like that. It wasn't too good a horn but it was mine and I loved it.

Uncle Emile kept schooling me and we would work and work until when my fingers got spread out a little I started on a B flat Albert-system clarinet. This was the real McCoy that all the clarinet players used in the bands. Sometimes in these early years when Ory's band had a ball to play, Emile would talk to my parents and take me along to sit in. I would stay on the stand with them as long as possible, which would be about an hour, until it got too late and I had to get home.

When I was starting to play music, we got together a group from among the neighborhood kids. A couple of the guys were trying to play instruments like trumpet and what not. We had a guy that was learning piano and another that was on drums and we tried to form a little group. We'd go around if anyone was giving a party and tell them we would play for a percentage of the gate. The price of admission would probably be 25 cents and we'd go there and play and go home with around a dime a piece by the time the night was over. We didn't care. We was having a ball and it was good for us. I enjoyed my life, especially when I got to play parades. I mean we would play from nine in the morning till around five at night for 75 cents, walking all over the city. I'd come home and my feet would be so sore and swollen that I'd have to put them in water. But I didn't care. I mean that's the only way I could learn, you know: try to learn, want to learn.

I wanted so badly to play with one of the good bands, but I knew that I would need to know a whole lot more on my horn before I could get to that stage. Of course a lot of the older clarinet men would try to encourage me. For instance there was a real fine player in New Orleans called Big Eye Louis DeLisle. He used to try to put work my way, even though he knew I was ill equipped to handle it right. I guess he must have sensed my enthusiasm or something. Anyway, he used to play at a place called "The Halfway House," and on Sunday afternoons they would have picnics to play. Big Eye was sometimes too tired to go and he would come and knock on my family's door and ask if I would play the picnic. Of course I'd say yes, even though I couldn't play worth a damn. The guys in the band would see me coming, especially the drummer Zutty Singleton, and he'd say, "Look who in the hell they sent out today." I had to go through all that experience but I didn't care. I had a hard face, so I just went out there and did the best that I could.

I knew that I needed another teacher other than my uncle because after all he was a violin player, not a clarinetist. I had a real good friend named Amos White who played trumpet and was a swell guy. I told him I was thinking of going to a teacher and I had been hearing so much about Alphonse Picou for one, and Lorenzo Tio for another. He told me that as long as I could afford the lessons that he would look into both these men for me.

At that time I was working days for a newspaper, *The Tribune*, as a photo engraver. I worked for an old guy named Romanski and made pretty good money. Especially if I worked overnight. We'd wait till they had an accident then take the picture and make cuts to put into the paper. I was around fifteen at the time. Therefore I could afford any lessons I was about to undertake.

Amos White had indeed been looking into teachers' credentials for me. He would try to help me best as he could because he was already himself an accomplished musician. We would sometimes run down some music together, and I'd be reading from the sheet and make a boo-boo and he'd got on my ass like white lightning to straighten me out. Anyway, I had mentioned to him about maybe taking some lessons from Alphonse Picou and he said, "On Monday we're going to go to the Lyric Theater where Picou is working with John Robichaux's Orchestra. We're going to go early and sit right behind Picou, because he always sits with his music stand facing towards the audience. I want you to watch him read his music. I couldn't see what he was driving at but come Monday we did just as Amos said and sat right directly behind Picou. After a few bars it became clear that that old man never played one part of that music and I asked Amos what was happening. "He's playing by ear," he said. "Well I'll be damned," I replied, comparing Picou with Tio. I was really disappointed with Picou and in later years I found out that he became famous just for that little part in *High Society*, and in fact he got that from one of Sousa's marches. That was all that made him famous.

On the other hand the first time that I heard Lorenzo Tio I was not disappointed at all. I heard him on a parade playing his A clarinet. He knocked me out right from the very start. My uncle promised me that he would take me to his house, as he knew him, and ask him to give me lessons. Meanwhile Amos White had landed a job playing at a "jitney" dance out at Spanish Fort. Lorenzo Tio was playing on the same nights as us at Tranchina's Restaurant at Spanish Fort. We would wind up before them each night so I would be able to go over to hear Tio play every night. What with this, and my uncle Emile's promise to approach Tio for lessons, I had a damned good year that year.

THREE

"The best damned clarinet player in New Orleans."

Uncle Emile had promised to take me to see Lorenzo Tio for lessons but it looked like he took his sweet time about it. I kept on asking him and he said, "Soon boy, soon." Meantime I started to watch for Tio, where he would play and all. I followed him all over the city of New Orleans. Anytime he would play a parade I would be right there listening to what he was making on that clarinet. Wherever he played I'd go and stand around the bandstand and all my listening was to the clarinet. I didn't care about the rest of it. If I heard a riff or something else that I liked, then I would hum it in my head, and keep humming it. I'd leave the dance and keep on humming it until I got home and no matter what time it was when I got home I would get out the horn and try to pick out the notes. I would keep on until I got it down right.

Finally my uncle told me one morning, "Come on. We are ready for Mr Tio." So he brought me over to Tio's house and rattled on the door. Tio's wife answered and told us her husband was sleeping. His wife understood these kinds of things because she was very familiar with the strange hours that musicians kept. She was the sister of Peter Bocage, who played alongside Lorenzo Tio in Piron's Orchestra. When her husband played with Piron at Tranchina's out at Spanish Fort, the orchestra played until three in the morning and afterwards most of the musicians would hang out at a place back in the city where they would drink and talk about this and that. Naturally, when they got home they went to bed and slept most of the day. Tio was at that time the best damned clarinet player in the city and that was his daily routine. He hardly ever had a night off.

Anyway they woke him and he came to the front of the house. "Mr Tio," my uncle says, "I would like for you to teach this boy the clarinet."

Tio says, "I have too many students now to fit them all in."

"But this boy is serious. He wants to be a professional clarinet player and learn his horn right. I wouldn't waste your time," says my uncle. Mr Tio looked at me for a long time and I guess he read something in my face. "OK, I'll teach him. Bring him back next week and we'll start."

Start we did. But slowly, slowly. The same procedure. His wife had to wake him, and that first lesson, it was very short. I remember he gave me about three notes to learn on the horn and that was it.

After the next couple of lessons we started to get down to the real stuff. I think maybe he was testing my attitude at first. Maybe he took me on just as a favor to my uncle. Certainly the 50 cents a lesson didn't mean a thing to him, but after a while he began to get more involved with my playing. It was strange, looking back now. Not like today where lessons might be $3 a half hour or anything like that. I mean, a lesson was 50 cents and that was for as long as he wanted. Not for as long as I wanted, but he wanted. Sometimes I'd be there for two hours or until he got tired. There was no set time, see. If I finished my lesson, he would go right on into the next one. I had to bring my *Lazarus Book* and we'd go through it page by page.

First I had to learn the scales, then the fingerings. Then he would explain tonation and have me hold a note without varying it. He didn't want me to vary it at all. It had to be one sharp or flat on strictly an even keel. We ran that stuff down a long while.

When we got to the chromatic scale, that was my toughest part. I had to start slow, then increase the tempo all the time, but I could never play it too fast. At last I got it together, but he still kept me at it so I asked him, "Why must I keep on doing this?" He said, "That gives your fingers the feel of all the keys of the instrument so when you begin to play your more difficult exercises, they won't be strangers to you."

Sometimes I thought I was doing pretty good and a couple of times I felt that I did great at his lessons, but he'd just say, "Fair." He did tell my folks though that I was doing pretty good and making progress. I think that he kept after me more than his other students because he liked me so much and he didn't want me to get a "swelled head" like a lot of the guys. Sometimes his pupils would learn to play two or three tunes and they'd never come back to him any more. That made him disgusted so he was all set to give me holy hell before anything like that would ever happen. He taught me a whole lot even for free, but, like I said, he would never admit to me that I was doing well. He would just nod and tell me, "It was pretty fair, but work harder at it. You can always do better."

He was a wonderful man. Quiet, very tall and distinguished looking with straight black hair and a copper-colored complexion. He played Albert system clarinet of course, but the old thirteen-key type, a little different from the one I use today. As I said, I never remember him having a night off. He was always in demand and in the daytime he would play parades or teach. Besides me he had several other pupils and, although he never mentioned their names, I found out that Albert Nicholas had been taking lessons from Tio before me. Albert was really far advanced and a fine clarinetist. Funny, although we both had the same tutor, we don't have the same style at all. He was also teaching Omer Simeon, and there's one of the real unsung clarinet players. Even though he had all these youngsters that he was teaching, he always took them singly—never two at a time or nothing like that. Also, he never had any white pupils. They were mostly all what you'd call Creole kids.

I almost forgot. He had another student who did very well named Peter DuConge. Peter came from a family of musicians. His brothers all played music. Peter did very well with Tio and in later years he went to Europe and married an American girl called "Bricktop" who was into the night-club stuff with Josephine Baker. He also played on some of those early records with Marlene Dietrich, so you know he was pretty good. Anyway, he finally got a divorce from Bricktop and before he died I heard he was somewhere around Minneapolis with a stable of race horses.

There was another guy named Sidney Vigne who was working out good with Tio, but he was killed under strange circumstances. It was on Christmas Eve and all the bands, when they finished work at night, would join up at a place called a "boudoir." This was during prohibition and there would be a pool room downstairs in this place and upstairs they would have food and drinks and whatever. Well, all the guys would meet there after hours and play pool and yap. Whoever lost at pool would have to buy the drinks all around. They would all drink this stuff called "Pink Lady" which was some kind of bathtub gin mixed with Grenadine. The bar would be lined up with bottles of this Pink Lady stuff by the time dawn came. Anyway, this guy was supposed to go to his mother's house for dinner on Christmas Day, but he kept dogs at his house. Maybe four or five of them. He was drunker than a hoot owl, but all that was on his mind was that he had to go home to feed his dogs before going to his mother's. His wife and kids were all over at his mother's house already when he left to go to the dogs. He got as far as Claiborne Street and was standing on the curb at the corner, waiting to cross, when along comes this big meat truck and one of the legs of a cow carcass was sticking out of the side. He didn't see it and it hooked alongside his head and threw him into the street in front of another truck. He was killed outright.

Somehow or other he had got hold of Albert Nicholas's union card, but that was the only thing he had on him besides his money. No identification at all. So when they took him to the morgue, they saw this card and figured that the guy was Nick. They took the address from the card and went right over to Albert's house. His wife came to the door and the cop told her, "Are you Mrs Nicholas? Well, I hate to tell you this, but your husband was just killed. I'm sorry."

"My husband's been killed! Well, it must have happened mighty quick because I just left him in the bed to answer the door to you." And Nick was there snoring like hell.

So, as you can see, Tio had his share of youngsters that were learning from him. Of course, there were other teachers around at that time such as George Baquet, who was teaching guys like Sidney Bechet and Emile Barnes. I remember as a little kid, when they'd play a funeral I would listen so hard to him with his E flat clarinet out there playing so beautifully that everyone cried.

They had another clarinetist, but nobody ever writes about the man. He was quite a musician, but he wasn't a jazz player. His name was Charlie McCurdy and he was quite a clarinetist but don't you know he couldn't improvise at all. I mean, nothing. It just wasn't in him. If you called *The Saints Go Marching In* in the key of F," unless you'd have something written for him he wouldn't play note one.

But Tio, now, that was a whole different ball game: he could transpose. He was a great reader, even by today's standards. He had real fast execution and he could improvise—play jazz in other words —on top of all the rest. He would even make his own reeds out of some kind of old cane. Yes, Lorenzo Tio was the man in those days in the city of New Orleans. But, as they say, all good things have to come to an end. That was how it was with me. Armand Piron's orchestra had an offer to go to New York and naturally Tio was with them, so he left town.

Before he went, he told me, "Barney, you look like you're going to make it, so I want to send you to my uncle Luis, my father's brother." I remembered Luis from Uncle Ulysses' cigar shop, so I changed teachers midstream. By this time I had quit working in the day, as I just wanted so much to be a musician. As money was a bit of a problem because I didn't work, I had to get my father to pay for my lessons with Luis "Papa" Tio. I had to fight him to get the money, but he came up with it after all my "hounding." I guess by then they all knew I was on my way with the horn.

Luis "Papa" Tio was a more patient teacher in a way than his nephew Lorenzo. He was also a hell of a clarinetist. He had a little symphony orchestra in a club he belonged to called "The Lyre Club Symphony Orchestra." He was the director and, believe me, he made plenty of enemies for a while. When some of the musicians made bad notes, he would tell them, "What's the matter? You keep making the same damn bad note. Can't you see it?" Then they would have an argument. He was a strict perfectionist as far as the drill went, and he was the same way as a teacher.

Just like Lorenzo, he played a thirteen-hole clarinet, but he had rubber bands all over it. Never mind the springs, I mean all over it. He even had some of the side holes stuffed up. But he could play all right. You see, his whole family were a line of clarinetists. One of them was first clarinet with Barnum and Bailey's Circus. I wish you could have heard old "Papa" play. I mean, he was fantastic!

When he took me on, he didn't really want to teach any more, to tell the truth. He had been teaching a couple of guys that he had got disgusted with. He was the type of man that if he thought there was no possibility of your becoming a clarinetist, he would tell you right off the bat. "Son," he would say, "I'm sorry, but you will never make it as a clarinetist, so why don't you try some other instrument. Try trumpet, or anything." That was the way he was. Just socked it to you.

By luck he must have taken a liking to me, because he told me I could go to him anytime I wanted. I would go there and just sit down and he would be talking of lots of things, for free. In fact, he knew I had no day job and when I couldn't afford to buy reeds he would make them for me for nothing from old cane he would cut down. Of course he still worked himself in the daytime. He was a cigar maker, but he would just quit work when he felt like it. Like, work half a day or something, then come home to be showing me stuff.

The biggest trouble I had was to play jazz, or "split time" as they call it. All my learning was from the book; if it was in four-four, then that's how I'd play it. Or three-four or whatever it was; two-four, six-eight, no matter what. But you see, all jazz is and was in split time, today and yesterday. In other words, you feel it as half the beats to the measure. It's not a time signature but just a feel. I had more trouble with that than with anything else since I began to play the horn. I could read the notes. After all, with all my learning that was nothing, just to read the notes. I just couldn't play them with a "cut" feel to give the music the swing and bounce that you need for jazz. But "Papa" Tio showed me how to do it. "When you get to playing in a jazz band, kind of think in two-four all the way, then you'll have it," he told me. "C'mon, let's practice it together," he would say. It took me forever, but I finally got it down.

I remember one time, while I was at that transitional stage, I was playing around picking up a few jobs with different bands to make out, and this guy named Octave "Oak" Gaspard came to my house. He used to pass by all the time and hear me practicing, so when he got stuck for a clarinet one day, he came to see if I would make a few of his jobs with him. He wanted me to try out and he had a rehearsal at his house. They pulled up *Tiger Rag* on me and by the time they got down to the theme, "Dat-da-da, Dat-da-da," I was way back at the front of the piece trying to make it in regular time. "What's going on? That's where you are supposed to have your break," Oak said. The trumpet player with them was Hippolyte Charles and he took pity on me and guided me through that *Tiger Rag*. He was a real nice guy to do that. But anyway, as I said, it was "Papa" Tio that finally got me to play in that jazz time.

I stayed with "Papa" Tio about four more years and then I went out for myself. He lived to be a pretty old man, and when he died in New Orleans the world lost a great clarinetist.

The one thing in my life that made me feel very proud happened around the time I was winding up with "Papa". Lorenzo had been back from working in New York with Piron and they were sent for again. Lorenzo didn't want to go for some reason, and he told Piron to take me. Piron, to my surprise, figured I could cut it and I was all set to go. He even brought the music to my house for me to study. I mean, all the clarinet parts. I felt for sure that I was going, but then Piron told me, "Lorenzo has decided to go," and I lost out on the traveling for a few more years.

One thing though that pleased me: Lorenzo thought that I was good enough to take over his star pupil for him. It was real funny for me to be teaching anyone but he did good, and although I don't have the patience for teaching I showed him everything that I could. His name was Louis Cottrell.

FOUR

"All down the line there
was music."

I had good teaching all right, but all the teaching in the world is no good unless you apply it to your work. I was lucky because, as I said, right from the start I could put into practice my knowledge as I gained it. Every time I would learn something new from Tio I could try it out that night in Amos White's band.

We held that jitney job out at Spanish Fort for a good while. That was really my first professional job with a band. The band played in a large ballroom for the jitney, or ten-cents-a-dance type of situation. You had to play one number right behind the last one and no more than two choruses each number. That let the owner sell tickets to dance with the girls. We packed the people in and they seemed to enjoy the band. I can't remember all the names of the guys but Amos White played trumpet, Charlie Bocage played banjo and Bob Ysaguirre played bass. Like I said, we were doing real good business until the white musicians out there got jealous. They didn't want a colored band doing all that business because it looked bad for them. So this Saturday night, when the place was crowded to the limit, they came and pitched a whole load of stink bombs into the dance hall. That ran the people out and it seemed to the owner that they wouldn't come back after that mess. He was sorry but he had to let us go before any real trouble started, and that was that.

After that gig closed I played around New Orleans with different bands. I played some jobs with Chris Kelly's band. He was a big guy from the country and very popular. No matter who would be in the band, as long as Chris would be there then the people would come. Most of the guys Chris would hire couldn't read anything but they could play fine together. Kelly himself was a fair trumpet player.

In those days most of the work was had by a name band. You take like Chris Kelly or Buddy Petit or Sam Morgan. They had most of the jobs sewn up. I can remember Sam Morgan real well. To me Sam was no sensational trumpet player, just mediocre, but he had a big name around town. His brothers all played music too. Andrew was the clarinet player, Isaiah played trumpet, but the best one was Al. He played bass, although he wasn't playing in New Orleans when I can remember. I didn't know anything about him until he came North. He was a fine, fine bass player.

One Labor Day I did my one and only gig with Buddy Petit's band. I'll never forget that job. We was out in the park playing like hell and the people was real happy. Everyone was having fun when up came this big cop. He walked right up to the bandstand and said, "Which one of you characters is Buddy Petit?"

Buddy spoke up with that stammer of his, "Y,y,yes sir. I,I,I,I'm B,B,Buddy Petit."

"Oh no," says the cop, "You can't be Buddy Petit. He's real famous."

"B,b,but I tell you that's me," says Buddy.

"You mean a little fellow like you is the great Buddy Petit that I keep hearing so much about," says the cop. "No. That just can't be."

By this time Buddy is getting kind of angry and insulted. "L,l,look. Here's my ID" he says. "Now don't that tell you who I am?"

"OK. You must be him for sure," says this cop. "You just put that horn in the case and come on down to the station with me. You're wanted for questioning." Man, he took Buddy away and we laughed like hell. We had to finish the job with no trumpet.

I think Edmond Hall was supposed to be with Buddy regular but he was sick that Labor Day. I never knew Edmond until later years. He came up to New York with Cootie Williams. They had a band out of Alabama. I think they called it "The Ross Deluxe Syncopators."

So I was spending a while just playing one night here and one there, listening to a whole lot of bands and practicing like mad. I always played an Albert system clarinet, and when the Boehm systems came out I just stayed with that Albert. Even today I prefer it. The Albert seems like it has a better tone to me.

Sometime around 1923 or early 1924 I met my first wife and we were married. Her name was Arthemise. With all this new responsibility I kind of wished that some regular job would come up. Sure enough, I didn't have long to wait.

Albert Nicholas, who I knew from being another Lorenzo Tio pupil, came to see me and offered me a job at Tom Anderson's place on Rampart Street and Canal. Anderson himself was one of those guys with the whole town in his pocket. He opened this place that was really just a glorified gyp joint. They had the main room and the band played at the back. There was always three bar tenders on duty and people would get anything they wanted in that place. They had plenty of girls too. Not whores but just, like, "B" girls. Always making the customers spend their "bread." Sometimes the place would get raided and when we would come up before the judge he'd ask, "Where are you from?" We would say, "Tom Anderson's," and he would say, "What the hell are you doing up here then? Get out of here right quick." We never got sentenced or anything because Anderson was a big shot in New Orleans.

The band was just called "Tom Anderson's Band" even though Albert Nicholas was really the leader. Arnold Metoyer played trumpet, Nick and I played alto and tenor respectively, Luis Russell was the pianist, Willie Santiago our banjo player, and Paul Barbarin played drums. He would just leave his drums there the whole day long and just come to work at night. I could walk to work from where I lived but sometimes I would catch the streetcar because it turned right outside the place. Sometimes Nick would get little outside jobs in the daytime, like for a couple of hours at one of the department stores. We played many Saturday afternoons at Maison Blanche for instance. They would use one of the store pianos and we'd play to attract the attention of their customers to some new product. We kept busy.

Around this time we had some trouble inside the family though. It was my brother Sidney. He was about twenty-six years old then and he had gotten married and left home. He got in a fight with some guy over his wife and he shot the guy. Sidney figured that that was the end of the thing and he got into his Model-T Ford he was driving, and the thing wouldn't start. He had to crank it, but when he took out the crank handle, he just threw his gun off the front seat. He was bent over the front cranking this car and the guy on the sidewalk started to get up. He wasn't injured so badly as they thought. He reached over the door and grabbed Sidney's pistol. Sidney saw he had the gun and ran into some lady's back yard. He was trying to get into the back door when the guy shot off the pistol and hit him in the arm. The bullet shattered the bones and they had him in the hospital. They told him that they would have to amputate his arm before gangrene set in. It was his right arm and he didn't want them to touch it. Sure enough, that gangrene set in right quick and that was it. He died right there in the hospital. My grandmother took it real hard but my father wasn't so upset. They just never seemed to get along, him and Sidney.

Anyway, Tom Anderson's place was still jumping. You know they had so many places right around that little area. All down the line there was music. Every tonk had a band. Just around the corner Peter DuConge had a band working for a guy called Beansie Fauria. That was on Iberville and Bourbon. Right down the street a couple of doors Tony Parenti had his band. A couple of blocks away Buttsy Fernandez had a place where Emanuel Perez and Udell Wilson worked. Perez played trumpet and Udell played piano. In fact he joined our band at Tom Anderson's when Luis Russell went to join King Oliver in Chicago. Buttsy Fernandez was quite a tough character. The sailors would always come into his place and start a fight. Buttsy would tell them, "Look here you sons-of-bitches, you think you can come in here and break up my place. Goddammit I'll break your heads and everything in them."

I think Albert and I had the best gig though, mainly because we had the best-looking girls in Anderson's. We weren't supposed to mix with the customers at all. We played for White only. We had our dressing room in the back and we couldn't go out front during intermission. The girls would take fifteen minutes rest and come back with us. At Mardi Gras all the girls would be in there with their masks on and they would all flirt with Nick and me. These girls took a liking to Nick and me and when the men would come in the place half drunk they would make them throw money in our "kitty" box. They all had their pimps that came in there regular to check on the cash flow from their outside activities. So anyhow I had this one girl that I was going with most every night. All the guys in the band warned me not to fool with her in case her pimp would find out. I was young. I didn't care.

She and I had this arrangement. She lived way uptown, a couple of blocks past St Charles Avenue going toward the river. She lived on the second floor and I would go out there every night when the job broke up. If the light was out, that meant come on up, but if the light was on, that meant her pimp was there so stay away. When I would leave Anderson's I'd take the streetcar to Lee Circle and have to change cars there, then get on another car and ride the five or six more blocks to where she lived at. I knew all the times of the streetcars by heart after a while and one night I got off the first one and was waiting for the second car when I saw this little car coming along with four or five guys in it.

I ducked behind a tree, because I didn't want no trouble that late at night, and as the car went past I heard them talking. "We're going to get that little son-of-a-bitch tonight and fix him good," I caught. It never dawned on me that it was me they were talking about. I had my tenor case with me. I used to bring it home every night. So here came the car and I got on, rode the six blocks and got off. I had to walk one block from where the streetcar set me down to where she lived. Here comes this same car with the five guys in it and I heard one holler, "There he is!" They went right past for a couple of yards. They were going too fast to stop, but as soon as I heard that "There he is" bit, there I wasn't. Man, I took off, and that tenor case felt like a feather to me. By the time they turned that car round I was long gone, with ease too.

After that little "humbug" I never did go to any girls' houses no more. I told Nick what happened. He was going with Jelly Roll Morton's sister at the time. She was working in the Ladies' Room at Anderson's and wasn't like the working gals. Anyway Nick and I rented this house under her name. That way we could bring whoever we wanted there with no trouble. We called it "The Play House."

Our music was going good at Tom Anderson's. Nick and I were quite a team. We had worked out a whole load of tight breaks on the two saxes and got some stuff together that no-one else in the city was doing. In fact sometimes the sax section of Fate Marable's band would come in and sit and listen to us play to pick up ideas. We had a lot of fun in that band. They were some real fine guys to work with.

The band had rented an old house that we called "The Kitchen," way back on Ursuline Street. Each weekend one of the guys would cook. We took turns at it. We had an old fashioned wine cooler back there and whoever did the cooking, well he had to fill that thing full of wine too. So this particular Friday it fell to our banjo player Willie Santiago to cook. He went across Claiborne Street somewhere and got him a whole great big red snapper. On his way back, the thing being so heavy with the fish and the wine, he stopped to take a rest. Now if you ever was down in New Orleans you may have heard about the "neutral ground." This was a big grassy patch with trees that ran all down Claiborne Avenue from Canal Street. It was like a great divider for the uptown and downtown traffic. Anyways, so Willie got to drinking that wine and got stinko. He fell asleep with the great big fish across his lap resting under a tree on the neutral ground. Naturally the sun was "catching" that snapper and when we finally found Willie he stank of fish for days. We never let him do the cooking after that.

We all got along pretty well in that band. The only guy that I didn't get too friendly with was Arnold Metoyer, and that was kind of my fault. Early on, when I joined the band, some people we barely knew took us out to hear Lorenzo Tio and Piron at Tranchina's. The guys in the band were all glad to see us and they kept feeding me wine. I never did have much of a head for wine, but this night I was loaded. When it came to go back into town I told Arnold to tell the people to let me sit in the jump seat. He didn't tell them nothing and so I sat up there with him. He wasn't much of a drinker, and I kept wanting to heave all the time on the trip back. I kept telling him to get them to stop, but he just said, "It's good for you. You ought to know better at your age. You won't heave." I held it as long as I could and then I just pulled open his jacket pocket and threw up right into it. What was I going to do? It wasn't my friends' car. We barely knew the people that took us out there and back. After that me and Arnold, we weren't so close.

Somewhere there is a photo published that I saw of that band. The funny thing is that all my horns are right there on the bandstand but I must have been in the men's room or something. I can see my tenor and my clarinet up there, but not me.

It's a funny thing about New Orleans. The bands and musicians are always trying to out-do one another or do something real different from anyone else. That's really why Nick hired me I guess. We were the only group in town with that instrumentation: two saxes. You talk about out-doing. I remember when I was a kid, Prof John Robichaux used to have the band at the Lyric Theatre. He had a drummer called Happy Bolton or "Red Happy" as he was known. Anyway, Happy gave old man Robichaux trouble so he got rid of Happy. Robichaux sent to Texas to get this real flashy drummer, whose name escapes me right now, but he was a sensation. So when show time came he got there early and arranged the pit. There was a great big space and he filled it with four or five galvanized tubs of different sizes. Then he took a great long string and hooked it up all along the wall right up into the "peanut gallery." He had a pistol arranged up there pointing upwards and loaded with blanks. It was nailed in the ceiling. The end of this string fitted around the trigger. So here came all the people and the band played the overture and turned loose this drummer. He went to banging on his drums then started hitting all these wash-tubs and climaxed the act by pulling the string and firing off the pistol way up in the peanut gallery. That really broke it up. They had never seen anything like that in New Orleans before.

In the same way they never saw anything like our "team of saxes." We had it going real good for a number of months but then business began to drop off a little. The boss had no alternative but let one of the saxes go. Now I'll tell you what I came to find out in those early years. Albert Nicholas was a sneaky character. See, unknown to me, he had had an offer to go to Chicago the week after the boss let me go. Nick knew all about the deal and it was all set and agreed with King Oliver. King was recommended by Luis Russell, who had left us earlier, to hire Nick, and Nick had agreed to it. When the boss gave me notice he should have spoke up right then and said, "Don't fire him. I'm going to leave anyway next week." But he didn't say shit and so I got fired and the next week Albert went to Chicago. That was a dirty trick and I never forgot it.

A few days after Albert quit this guy who had just fired me came to my house and pleaded with me to come back. He offered me a good raise and so I did go back. When I went back to work that week at Anderson's they had made Paul Barbarin the nominal leader but it was really anybody's band. Things were never the same on that job after I went back. I must have stayed on for a month or so until one day when I got home my grandmother told me there was a cable that had come for me. In those days if a cable came, it was something big. I mean some of the houses even had telephones but we didn't have one, and so this cable was a real big deal. The postmark read, "Chicago, Illinois." I trembled with excitement as I tore it open. It was from King Oliver. He wanted me to join him as soon as possible in Chicago. I sent him back a cable and then we agreed the salary and he sent me my ticket. I was kind of glad to be getting out of New Orleans in a way. In fact, I would have probably joined anyone's band just to make a trip North, but in those days very few musicians ever got a cable from King Oliver.

FIVE

"He was the King all right."

When I was leaving New Orleans—it was just around Christmas time 1924—my grandmother, bless her soul, brought me to the railroad station. She made me put on three suits of long underwear. "It's going to be so cold up there. I don't want you to catch a cold and get sick," she said. "And keep your overcoat on at all times too," she hollered as the train pulled out. I rode all by myself on the "coach" up to Chicago. I had to sleep on the seats and "rough it on up" as they used to say. As that old train pulled out of New Orleans it would be many years and many miles before I would see my home town again.

King Oliver met me at the station in Chicago, but I had a bad fever and was shivering all the ride back into town. When I finally got to see a doctor he told me, "No wonder you caught cold with all that under-wear, perspiring all the time." From that day on I always wore shorts.

I found out that it had been Luis Russell who suggested to Joe Oliver to send for me, and Albert Nicholas had kind of seconded the motion. The only thing was that when I got to Chicago, there was no work. The place we were supposed to play in was the Royal Gardens and, as luck would have it, the place had burned down two days before New Year's Eve. Nobody knows to this day what caused the fire, but since it was the holidays and the place was all decorated, they just figured that something caught fire and away went the Gardens. That left the band without a job. The band when I arrived was King Oliver and Bob Shoffner on trumpets, George Filhe on trombone, Albert Nicholas and Darnell Howard on clarinets and saxes, Luis Russell on piano, Bud Scott on banjo, Bert Cobb on bass, Paul Barbarin on drums, and I played just tenor and soprano sax. That was a wonderful band, but without a job we knew we were in for a hell of a time. "Welcome to Chicago" the signs over town read, but even so I was just happy to be there.

Albert Nicholas and I took a room together and we made out all right,

I guess. I had friends up there. I mean, I had a cousin named Natty Dominique who was living in Chicago, and Jimmie Noone helped me quite a bit. Then there was a one-legged piano player named Richard "Myknee" Jones that used to get a few gigs and also Alma Hightower; she was the wife of trumpet player Willie Hightower. The secretary of the Musicians Union would also send us on little jobs just to help us over this bad patch. These kinds of jobs wouldn't want two reeds, so Albert and I would flip a coin and whoever won would take the gig. Whatever money we made we put together and split on food and rent like.

Things began to break for the band when Joe Oliver was offered the matinee at a place called the Plantation. A guy called Dave Peyton already had the band there, and he was in charge of all the music. Anyway we took the matinee job and had a rehearsal that first morning. We played the job and the man that owned the place liked us so much that he started to talk business with Joe. That made Peyton real mad. I mean, he already had another job but it looked like he wanted to corral the whole damn business. Seeing as how he wrote the music for the whole show, top to bottom, he found an easy way to get us out of there. At least so he figured. He would write the music so hard that he knew Joe couldn't cut it, but Joe was smart and he hired different guys who could play all that hard stuff to play lead. That's the way we got along.

After a couple of months things had changed around and Joe had our band billed as The Dixie Syncopators as top attraction at the Plantation. Those were good days. We had our own book and we would play all those things like *Eccentric Rag* and *Royal Gardens Blues* just as Joe liked to play them. For all the people that wanted to dance, well, we played all the hit tunes of the day like *Animal Crackers* and so forth. They had those long orchestrations they pull out for all that kind of stuff.

Joe Oliver was quite a guy and he would love to kid a lot. I remember one night when we were playing *Eccentric Rag*, and Bob Shoffner—he was real dark, you know—would get mad at Joe kidding all the time on the band stand. So Joe took his mute—he was a master with that mute—and told Bob, "Here's how a white baby cries: 'Oooh, oh, oooh, ohwa'" from that mute. "Now, here's how you cried when you were a baby, you big black so and so: 'Wah, wah, wah, wah.'" All the band broke up so they could hardly play, but Bob didn't see anything funny in it. They was a card, those two. Just like Frick & Frack. Oh, it was something else.

Joe would kid all the time, on the stand and off, until one day something happened to change all that. He would always tell the "dozens" as they called them. In other words, nasty things about your family such as, "Your mother's so big, she has to have a tent for a Kotex," and stuff like that. Anyhow, Joe had such big feet, big, bad feet with fallen arches and all. I would be kidding about his feet and he would lay the dozens on me about my family. So one night he came in and I started to kid him about the feet. He started to get evil, then turned and walked off. Later, when he cooled off a little, he said, "Don't kid me no more. I had a dream and my mother told me not to tell the dozens ever again." That was how he was. He just stopped all that stuff and never mentioned it again. His mother had been dead for many years and he figured it was some kind of omen.

But to get back to that stuff he did with the mute. I mean, I never saw anyone in my life use mutes the way he did. To get that stuff out of a horn. I guess that's why they called him "King" Oliver. The way we got along I called him anything I wanted to, but he was the King all right. For instance, there was a guy in Chicago called Paddy Harmon who was a big businessman. He owned a great big ballroom too. He and his associates used to come to the club all the time to see Joe and what he was doing with that mute. Then later, that's how they came out with the "Harmon" mute: the metal mute with the cup on the end. Joe used to do the same thing with two fingers holding this tiny mute in between them and work it like nobody's business. He was something else.

Joe as a band leader was really a guy that could get the best out of his men. There was no pressure with him, but you know, I used to feel sorry for him, because he had pyrrhoea. Sometimes he would come in at night to blow his horn and his teeth would go all the way back in his mouth. Nothing much would come out of his horn on those nights. As he got older it got worse. But he was never hard on his sidemen. I mean, he didn't want any fooling around. All he asked was that you do your work. He didn't want any playing around, unless he did it. And he really did it to keep up the guys' spirits. For instance, he would never stay apart from the men in the band. Like, they would be at one hotel and he would be right there in that same hotel with them. He was always close to the band and the guys respected him for that. After all, it's not like nowadays. The guys in those days were getting a salary, which incidentally was the same amount for everyone in Joe's band, and they respected the leader for that pay. Nowadays they don't even respect that pay. They show up high or stoned or sometimes don't even show up at all. They don't even care. And Joe was good financially too. Whatever he told you you would get, that's exactly what you would get.

Joe was just as nice off the stand as on it. He was a big guy, weighing around 240 pounds. I never saw him take a drink. Now, I'm not saying he never drank, just that I never saw it. But he would eat to make up for that. He had a lovely wife named Stella. She was real nice and used to cook for the guys sometimes. She never went on the road with Joe, but stayed home in Chicago. I don't know what became of her after Joe died. Last thing I heard, she was living out in California some place. Joe would just sit around all day and eat her cooking. Then he would go to work and after the job he would go eat again.

Every night when we finished at the Plantation, he would go maybe with a couple of the guys in the band to a Chinese Restaurant on State Street. There was a bakery on the way and he would stop and pick up this great big loaf of warm bread, and he would tuck it under his arm. We'd go into this Chinese place and we'd order food. Joe would order a big pot of tea. He would dunk his bread into the Chinaman's tea and use up all his sugar. The poor Chinaman couldn't figure out where all the sugar was going, but after a while he got wise and would hide the sugar, Joe would say, "What kind of restaurant do you call this? No sugar? I'm going to take my business elsewhere!"

He was really a "safe" man as far as spending money went, but he was at heart a good guy and I liked him. He would never knock anyone. He never discussed the guys that were in his band before us in any bad way. In fact, quite the opposite. He was crazy about Louis Armstrong and Louis was crazy about him. They were like father and son. Until the day he died, Louis thought that the sun rose and set on King Oliver. You see, Joe had sent for Louis to come up from New Orleans to play second trumpet in his band, just like he sent for me, but Louis really won the people where they worked at the Lincoln Gardens, or Royal Gardens as it became later. But Joe had never really let Louis go for himself. I mean, they would have that rapport that the books write about with the two horns, where Joe would lean over and play the notes to Louis of a "break" that was coming up. After two hearings, Louis would have it and then they made it together in the next chorus. That's all history now anyway.

What really started Joe into giving Louis his own chorus, and this is what Joe Oliver told me, was that one night they were playing when this guy Johnny Dunn walked in who was cracked up to be a hell of a trumpet man in those days. Johnny Dunn was with a big show and the people were clamoring to hear what he would play. He walked on to the stand and said to Louis, "Boy! Give me that horn. You don't know how to do." That made Joe Oliver real angry and he told Louis, "Go get him." Louis blew like the devil. Blew him out of that place. They looked for Johnny Dunn when Louis finished but he had skipped out. They never found him in there again. So that's when Joe started to turn Louis loose by himself.

Some time towards the end of 1926 things around Chicago were getting real bad with the gangsters and so on. I remember one night at the Plantation. You see, Joe Glaser, he had the Sunset right across the street from us, and he was somehow tied in with the gangsters. We were taking all the business from him, so one day these gangsters were up on the roof of the Plantation. They were planting bombs all over the roof, and of course people saw them up there in the broad daylight but just figured they were up there to fix a hole, I guess. Even the people who lived next door in the apartment paid them no mind.

So that night we were sitting around before work. You know, Albert Nicholas had been in the Navy and was on one of those submarine chasers. I asked him, "Weren't you afraid out there in the water with all those charges falling all around?"

He told me, "No, you just don't give it a thought. With the boat going like mad, all the explosions seem like nothing."

"I'd give it some thought," I said. "I wouldn't want to be around all that noise".

Albert just said, "Oh! You get used to it."

The first set started and we were playing *Animal Crackers* when "VROOM!" Debris started falling everywhere. I was stunned. I didn't know what was going on. Then another shot. "VROOM!" Right over the band stand. A guy came running up to the bandstand hollering, "Play, play!" It seemed like my horn was playing itself. The whole place was in a turmoil. Everyone was scrambling to get out. The people were running to the vestibule to get outside when another one hit the front of the place. I took off like a bat out of hell and went home. When I got there Nick was in bed quaking. "What happened? I thought you got used to all that stuff?" I said. Those were rough days. Oh God, they were rough!

Later that same year I guess Nick had enough because he left the band and went to China. They wanted me to go but I was happy in Chicago and my wife was pregnant too. In fact, she went home to New Orleans and had a son whom we named Barney Jr. Later, while she and

I were in New York, we had three daughters: Winifred, Marlene and Patricia. After that my wife and I kind of just drifted apart. I was on the road so much. Joe hired Junie Cobb to take Albert's place and he worked out pretty good. Darnell Howard left around the same time to go out to the Orient also, and Joe got Omer Simeon to replace him.

After they bombed the Plantation, it seemed like things was going from bad to worse and Joe was getting disgusted. You see, at that particular time they had two unions in Chicago: one white and one colored. James Petrillo, he was the head of the white local, and somehow he was tied into that gangster bunch. They had a boundary line where Negroes couldn't work, but the white musicians could just go and work anywhere they wanted. That made it tough for us. If we tried to take a job in a white place then Petrillo would send the goons in. These characters would tell the owner, "We're going to bomb you all out." And they did it too.

So Joe Oliver figured there was no way to get ahead in Chicago, and in addition they had a guy that was supposed to be going to book us all the way through to New York, so we had a meeting and decided to leave Chicago and go out on the road. Junie Cobb didn't want to go, so while we were out on the first leg of the trip Joe sent to New Orleans and got Paul Barnes to join the band.

We were supposed to open the tour in St Louis and carry right on through to New York. We had to get to St Louis the best way we could. We didn't have any band fund or much personal money so we got there the cheapest way we could: by train, boxcar style. That was one hell of a tour! We got to St Louis and we opened for this guy, Jesse something or other. He turned out to be the biggest crook. He just up and took off with all the money after the job closed. Joe had to break it to the guys in the band that there was no payroll coming. They took it real hard, but Joe just took it in his stride. He had this booking agent, and he had confidence in the guy. Much more than the guy had in him. He was always telling Joe, "Oh, don't worry. We're going to get this." Then, after we didn't get it, it would be, "Oh, we'll get that instead."

Joe figured that it would all be OK when we got to New York so we went on that hard-times train again until we got to the Big Apple. We opened at the Savoy Ballroom in New York City and the crowd loved us. We packed the place that first week. We could have played there for two or three months, but this damned booking agent guy told Joe, "We can do better." That made Joe ask them for a whole lot more money. They couldn't make it so they let us go.

We went out on the road again, and finally got stranded in Baltimore, Maryland. It was in Baltimore that we were booked for a short series of dances, but what happened to finally break the camel's back was this: the band was late getting to the first dance, and by the time we got there around two-thirds of the people had gone away disappointed at having no band. We played for the last part of the dance and the boss claimed that he lost money and wouldn't pay us. In a couple of days, they had another dance but none of the band would go because of what happened last time. Later we heard that the place was packed and jammed. It just seemed that everything was going against us the whole time.

While we were in Baltimore figuring out what to do, Omer Simeon had an offer to join Charlie Elgar's band in Milwaukee and he left us. We were really in some bad shape. I had about 40 cents in my pocket, so I made out by eating a hot dog every day. They cost around a nickel then. We stayed at some woman's house who had a large place with some extra rooms. The guys were all ganging up, rooming together. Joe was just like the rest of us: broke.

Finally, Joe managed to scrape together enough money to get the band back to New York and then the guys just spread out. Most of them had chicks there helping them, feeding them and that sort of business. That's what they call the "good old days!" Man, those "good old days" were as tough as anything!

Meantime good old Omer Simeon was with Charlie Elgar in Milwaukee and he told Mr Elgar about me. He was from New Orleans too, Charlie Elgar. A violinist in fact. He'd heard about me and I had heard about him, but we had never met. He made me an offer and even though it broke my heart to leave Joe Oliver, and as much as Joe was begging me to stay, I just couldn't. I had to feed my family. So I went to work for Charlie Elgar.

Joe kept the band going for a while I heard later, but finally he went somewhere South to rest. I believe it was Savannah. He kept his hand in with the music business for the next few years, and sometimes got a band together for a tour, but it was never the same. Just like the spirit had gone out of him.

The last time I saw Joe was in later years, when I was playing a dance in Savannah with Duke Ellington. He came to the place to hear us play. He looked just the same apart from the fact that his teeth were all gone. He seemed to be holding up all right. I mean, for one thing, he was immaculately dressed. Oh, he was happy to see some of his old friends!

He said that Louis had been good to him and sent him money to help out from time to time. He had no plans to come back into the music and wasn't doing anything much, at least that he cared to tell us about, but he was eating and sleeping. We laid some cash on him and it made him feel good. Like I said, he was immaculately dressed and in my mind he still *looked* like the King, even if he didn't have a palace and a court to prove it too.

SIX

"Oh! That music."

It was the summer of 1927 and things were looking up when I walked
into the Eagles Ballroom that first night to take the stand with Charlie
Elgar's Orchestra. Charlie was a violinist originally from New Orleans
who had been in Milwaukee for years. In fact he had held down a job at
a place called "The Roof Garden" for a long time when he first got to
Milwaukee but then he tired of it and went to Chicago and became an
official in the Musicians Union. An executive in fact. He wasn't satisfied
with that for long and took to hankering for Milwaukee once more. He
moved back there and took the job at the Eagles.

It was a big ballroom and we worked there on Friday, Saturday and
Sunday every week from eight to twelve. The Eagles was some big
fraternity like the Masons, see. I stayed there all that summer for the
whole season. You see, Mr Elgar, he was so nice to me because I was
really down those last few days with Joe Oliver. But Mr Elgar heard of
my predicament and gave me a lump sum of money so I could get back
into operation again. He then took a little out of my salary each week
until we drew even on the deal.

The orchestra was a little larger than I had been used to and ran to
twelve pieces. It was strictly a reading band with arrangements and all.
The material we played was written for us by some piano player that
lived around there. You see Mr Elgar didn't play anything in the
orchestra. He was strictly a front man and the people loved him. He
was a true diplomat, let's say.

Omer Simeon and I were the only New Orleans musicians in the
band. I soon made myself acquainted with the rest of the guys but
Simeon was my buddy. I stayed at his folks' house in Milwaukee. You
know, that man was a real unsung hero of jazz music. He was such a
quiet man, real quiet, but he could play like hell. He was an excellent
reader too. The funny thing about Omer, if the band went to check in at
a hotel in any of the towns we played, he would go to the YMCA. I

guess to save money. His wife was from Milwaukee and she always wanted to be part of that Chicago "smart set." I remember one time in later years when I was with Duke Ellington, I could have gotten Simeon into Duke's band. Ellington was just about to fire Otto Hardwick on account of his unreliability. He would go off for three or four days and no one would know where he was. So Duke got tired of that and was going to "can" him. I had the job all cut out for Omer but his wife talked him out of it. She wanted him to go back to Chicago to be in society. Later when we played Chicago with Duke and she saw how good we was doing and how he could have made some money she called me over from the bandstand at intermission and stooped over and said, "Go ahead. Kick me in the butt." I told her, "Why should I do it? Your husband ought to."

Anyway, so I was doing pretty good with Charlie Elgar and one day he told us that he was sending to New Orleans to get Emanuel Perez to play trumpet with us. That was about a month after I joined the band and I was happy about the deal. Manuel had been in Chicago a few years before and he was pretty hard to get out of New Orleans. They had a funny thing down there. Guys hated to leave their home and all that business. Elgar knew what he could do and how fantastic Manuel was, and so he sent for him. Next thing you know he must have caught Manuel at a good time because here he appeared in Milwaukee and stayed all summer too.

He roomed with us at Simeon's mother-in-law's house. That was great because we would practice a lot together in the day times. Manuel Perez taught me a great deal. Mostly Manuel and I would practice together, but sometimes Omer would join us. We would run down studies and reading, and then Manuel was showing me how to transpose. You see Emanuel Perez was not one of those "fly" trumpet players that you have today. He was very tasty, a thorough musician.

Another strange thing about New Orleans musicians. They have a sort of in-built tradition that if you are in a band away from home then you are supposed to take care of them and all that stuff. Even though they are big boys they sort of think you should go everywhere with them and that used to work on my nerves. The best thing about Omer and Manuel was that they weren't at all like that. I mean we would bum together because we got along. In most cases I seem to get along better with strangers than I do with people from my own home town, but in this case it was different.

We had a lot of fun that summer playing with Mr Elgar. We would play for dancing but as the season progressed it got more free on the bandstand. At first he would call all the tunes but after he got to know his men a little better he would ask you for suggestions. He also broke the group down and featured a solo guy with the rhythm section and the whole band playing "comp." I played tenor and soprano and Omer played alto and mostly clarinet. Its funny all the studying I had done to master the clarinet yet I hadn't really played it so much since I left New Orleans. I mean I played tenor with Joe Oliver and tenor with Elgar. I was self-taught on tenor and yet here I was making all my living on tenor and not clarinet.

On my feature numbers I would take the sax and slap-tongue the hell out of it. Many years before, in New Orleans, Piron's old alto player Louis Warneke had shown me how to get that sound like knocking on wood from the slap-tongue effect. A lot of those gimmicks, or tricks, in music originated with the old-timers in New Orleans. Like for instance that thing drummers do when they pick up the snare drum and scream through it. Paul Barbarin would do that all the time with King Oliver on *Tiger Rag*. When they would hit the "Hold that tiger" strain he would hold up that drum and "Whooooo, that tiger."

But anyway, I was the slap-tongue king in those days with the tenor because my tongue was so strong. What caused me to quit all that was that I broke so many reeds. At that time reeds singly would run around 75 cents and I would buy a box and maybe get one really good reed out of the whole lot, then go to slapping on it in the heat of the moment and then I'm in trouble. After a while I cut it out and forevermore left the gimmicks to someone else. I had better need of my cash. I thought to myself, "Well, it feels good to be eating again," and "Oh! That music."

You understand, we worked three nights a week at the Eagles Ballroom and then Mr Elgar would book us all around the area for maybe two more nights. Places like Racine and Madison. This meant we had a night or two off every week and would just go down to Chicago and dig all that good jazz music.

There was just too much to cover at that time. Johnny Dodds was there with his brother Baby Dodds, Jimmie Noone, Freddie Keppard, Earl Hines. Oh! I tell you that was some year. Manuel, Omer and I would drive down to Chicago and stay the night and come back next day. Jimmie Noone was working with Keppard in Charlie Cooke's Orchestra and we would dig them for a while until the end of their show then we'd go off to a place called "The Nest" that was an after-hours joint that Jimmie worked in. To get back to Doc Cooke: that was a devil of a band. They had three trumpets, four saxes, Jimmie on clarinet, three trombones, bass and two drummers. Doc himself played organ and he had the whole band arranged on like a stepladder with his organ down on the center of the floor. Jimmie was the main one for me. I really like his style. In fact I stole a whole lot from Jimmie. While he was playing with Charlie Cooke he mostly played harmony parts or whatever they had written on the paper for him, but after at The Nest he played mostly lead all night because the band was so small.

He was a great person outside of music too. He would take me to his house to eat sometimes. His wife was a good cook. He was a friendly guy, always laughing and smiling. He never actually showed me anything, but, like I say, I stole a lot of his licks. About a year or so later he made those fantastic records with Earl Hines and Joe Poston and I always enjoyed playing those.

Johnny Dodds was another thing altogether. We would go down to Kelly's Stables to listen to his group. His brother Baby played drums and my cousin Natty Dominique played trumpet. Natty was Don Albert's uncle. Whatever Johnny played was good but I don't think he could read at all. He was a little what you might call "limited." But what he played was good. He by no means ever impressed me like Jimmie Noone did. Manuel and Omer liked Johnny's little band very much but they never really passed any remarks about the music. In those days you would never dream of asking to sit in and play with another band. Kelly's Stables was a real small place that was inhabited mostly by whores, pimps and gangsters. It was Johnny's job and we always liked to go there. He and Baby, his brother, seemed to get along real good. Baby was a little hard to get along with for anyone but his brother. I guess he respected his brother so much. As a drummer he was really great. I never actually worked with him myself but he was a terrific showman, especially with a big band. Quite naturally, when he was with Johnny's little group he couldn't do all of his show stuff, but he was still sensational.

They had a lot of good drummers around that time in Chicago. For one, there was Tubby Hall. That's Minor Hall's older brother. I played a few jobs with him and he was real solid. He was much more steady than his brother. I mean Ram was sometimes good and sometimes he wasn't. That sort of thing. They also had a great drummer in that time called Clifford Jones. He had only two teeth and so the people called him "Snags." He would really go into his act. He would put the sticks under his arms, through his teeth, bang them on the floor and catch them. He was a sensation and he taught all that stuff to this drummer living today called Sylvester Rice. You know one thing? All those good drummers seemed to come from good old New Orleans.

That was when I first met Jelly Roll Morton: around Chicago. Now there was a man. The guy could write more tunes than anybody you could think of. Like if he needed money he would sit at the piano and compose a tune right there and then and take it to his publisher Mr Melrose and get maybe a thousand dollars as advance royalties. He did some great stomps you know, and in fact Jelly always claimed that he wrote *St Louis Blues* and that W. C. Handy stole it from him. He may have been right. Who knows? I mean the guy wrote so much great stuff anyway. I never knew him in New Orleans, but I knew his sister very well. She used to work in the Ladies' Room of Tom Anderson's where I worked. Albert Nicholas used to go with her around that time too.

So, the season was coming to the close and what an enjoyable time it had been for me. I wish I had gotten to record with the band that Charlie Elgar had. They had made some records a couple of years before Manuel, Omer and I were with them, and in fact some of the guys that were in that earlier band that recorded were still in the band with us. Guys like I remember Harry Swift the trombonist, and Lawson Buford the bass player.

Towards the last part of that summer I had a letter from my old buddy Luis Russell. He wanted me to come to New York to join him. I thought about it a lot. Mostly because of my unhappy memories of being there with King Oliver I almost declined, but at the last minute I changed my mind and told Mr Elgar I was going to leave. He was very sorry to lose me and I heard later that Manuel Perez had left the band real soon after me and gone home to New Orleans. Meantime there I was, all by myself again, riding the train. I wondered what would become of this trip?

SEVEN

"Give the Apple one more crack."

It was funny thinking back. I had worked with Luis Russell on and off for five years or so and we always did get along, and here I was bound once more for New York to join his band. I thought to myself, "I'm just going to give the Apple one more crack." Luis had left Joe Oliver just after I had and he had gone to New York to take an offer to work at a place called the "Nest Club" for a drummer named George Howe. After three months or so the owner decided to make Russell the leader and that was how he came to have his own band. Not only did he have his band at the Nest but he was also in charge of the subsidiary band at Small's Paradise. The main band there was led by a guy by the name of Charlie Johnson.

When I got to New York Russell was real glad to see me and I soon fell in with what they were doing. Paul Barbarin was also in the band at the time I was, and so there was three of us from our first little band at Tom Anderson's in New Orleans. Luis and Paul had done alright for themselves in the business, for like me they had both gone to play with King Oliver, and here they were doing good business and making nice money in New York. Neither of them had changed much since the days at Tom Anderson's.

Luis was the same beautiful man to work with or for. I've never seen a nicer man to work for in my life. He was always smiling and never, but never, got angry over anything. He didn't have any big ideas of his own importance. He was a terrific piano player too, and a great musician. He knew music, I guess, from his studies. I mean he never needed an arranger like, for instance, Charlie Elgar did. Luis Russell always did his own stuff for his band. With his own playing, well, he always liked to "feed" a man with chording, and always the correct chords at that. He liked to give a man good rhythm. He might make a little figure, you know, but none of this running all over the piano the way I know that a lot of pianists do. I mean he'd chord you all the way round. He never cared much about taking solos either.

I have read in books that this little band we had was the prototype of the later famous Luis Russell band, the one that made all those records. People said that our group was like a springboard for his ideas that he would use later. Now that just wasn't so. We had a different set-up altogether. We didn't have any what you might call "heavy" arrangements like he used later. In other words the small band had much more leeway than the later big orchestra. We could play more improvised stuff like, for instance, the way he had our group set up; if you wanted to take a solo or extend a solo, you could do it. Nothing was spoiled. In his later band you had "spots" and that was it. Some of the numbers he used were the same kind. I can remember that he used to feature some of his own stuff. *Mumtaz* was one of his own compositions that we played a lot at the Nest. He was the easiest man in the world to work for. No problems.

That bandleading isn't no easy thing. I mean Russell was a bandleader that everyone in the band loved and respected. He didn't argue with you. He just told you what he wanted and he always got what he wanted. I mean if you didn't like it you could always quit. Nobody quit while I was with him though.

Now my other friend from New Orleans days with the band was Paul Barbarin. I want to tell you a little about Paul. His playing had never changed from the days at Tom Anderson's. He was a good drummer; a good, solid drummer. He wasn't any soloist to speak of. I mean he could play a solo. Not like these guys of today do but really his beat was solid "beat" stuff. I know a lot of guys, like when they would get into a big-name band like King Oliver's, then they would change and their heads would get all swelled up. But not Paul. He was the same guy as when I first met him.

I had met Paul Barbarin way before the days that we played together at Tom Anderson's. He had been to New York in some show. I think it was *The Blackbirds*, or something like that. So when he came back to New Orleans he had no place to stay. My folks had a little place in back of our house and so they rented it to Paul and his wife. Then we became acquainted. He was five or six years older than I was but we became friends. I used to whistle a lot and he would beat his sticks on our front stoops. When I began to play an instrument, and I mean I really couldn't play nothing on it, Paul would help me a whole lot by beating time for me with his sticks, and we got along real well. Naturally I was glad when we worked together at Tom Anderson's and then in Oliver's band. Paul was the same friendly guy on the stand as he was off it and I loved to work with him.

It's a funny thing, that on and off the stand business. I mean some guys are so different. Take Zutty Singleton for instance. Now Zutty is a fine drummer and I love him, but he is pretty hard to work with. If you're not in a band with Zutty he is the greatest guy in the world, but in a band he's like a "Jekyll and Hyde" character. It's on account of his disposition. I never worked with Zutty after we left New Orleans except on a couple of record dates, but I remember when I worked with him down there in a band he would say, "Oh my! They sent us a snake charmer today." I was real mad but I had a hard face. It's funny because in later years we have become good friends and we would call him long distance and he would call us and gab for an hour or so. I was really upset when he died. We played a benefit for him with our trio "The Pelican Trio" and I was so glad to do it for him. They made a load of speeches from the stage all about him and I knew I had lost a good one.

But to get back to Luis Russell's band. After I had been at the Nest for a couple of weeks this guy that was the main man at Small's Paradise he wanted me to leave Russell and go with him. I wouldn't do it. I mean we made the same salary at both places but the tips at the Nest were tremendous; plus the fact I enjoyed working with Russell so much. We had six pieces at the Nest: Russell, Paul Barbarin and myself, then another sax player, trumpet and bass. I can't remember the guys' names but they were all from New York I think. We only ever rehearsed about three times total. I mean we just had no time. We were working all the while.

See the Nest was a real after-hours place where all the show girls from the Cotton Club, where Duke Ellington was working, would come after work and bring their boy friends. They enjoyed themselves like mad and everyone spent plenty of money in that little joint. People would come from the Broadway shows and practice what they called "slumming" at our place. They'd come down to our Nest and have a ball. Many real famous Broadway entertainers would come there too. I remember people such as Fanny Brice, Bill "Bojangles" Robinson, Helen Morgan and that guy that made *The Grapes of Wrath* named James Barton. Al Jolson would come there a lot and give the band money to keep us blowing. We made more money at the Nest in tips than the salary paid. Sometimes we would stay so long I'd get home like around noon or two, maybe three, in the afternoon. Not all of the band would stay after hours but Russell, Paul and I did. We were used to those long hours from our New Orleans days. We were young, we could take it. It was left to the guys in the band if they wanted to make that overtime tips money. Luis Russell never forced them to stay and work, although we always had at least four of us stay. Sometimes the whole band stayed.

The manager of the Nest was a guy named Jeff Blood. I'll never forget when I started I couldn't get used to the way those New Yorkers talked. One night this Mr Blood came up to me and hollered in my ear, "Come on boy. Get off." I figured he meant get off the stand so I started packing. I thought he was firing me, but Russell said, "What's happening? Where are you going?"

"The man told me to get off," I said. Russell explained to me that that was the slang way they used to tell you to take another chorus or blow, blow until you hit your high spots. It broke the band up. They laughed and laughed.

Those were times I'll never forget, but certainly there was one night that I'll never ever, ever forget. That was the night we had a visit from a bass player called Wellman Braud that was to change my whole life. If Braud hadn't have walked into the Nest that night maybe this book would never have been written.

EIGHT

"I started that Friday and ended fourteen years later."

I didn't know Wellman Braud that night when he walked into the Nest, and he didn't know me. He had heard about me through King Oliver and that was about it. He just sat there not talking to anyone until intermission came and then he asked me to join him at a table. He introduced himself and right away I knew he was a "home boy" from the way he spoke. Anyway, he told me that he could get me into the Duke Ellington Band, if I wanted. I just let him keep talking. "You see," he said, "Duke has had this six-piece outfit on Broadway, but he has just landed this deal at the Cotton Club. The man there wants him to expand the band to ten pieces." I kept listening. "Duke wants to get a clarinet player to take the place of Rudy Jackson. He is kind of tired of Rudy." I just sat there with my drink and let Braud go on talking. "Rudy came to Duke with this song he called *Creole Love Call* and Duke liked it and recorded it for Mills. Now it turns out that Rudy stole the damned song from King Oliver. Oliver used to call it *Camp Meeting Blues*, but Rudy claimed it was his original so Oliver is suing them. Duke has had enough of it all so he wants someone to take Rudy's place." I guess I couldn't blame him for getting rid of a guy that brought on so much trouble to his band. I mean, nobody needs law suits.

I wasn't interested in all the intrigue of why he was going, but Braud stayed with it and told me about how the band was getting ready to break into the big time and all. He claimed he would bring Duke down after a night or so to hear me. I told him, "Fine." That seemed to be that.

I had seen Duke before, but I had never ever met him. They used to have a place at that time in New York called "Mexico's" which was an after-hours spot that musicians would go to. They used to have music contests—"cutting contests"—there between the musicians. One night it would be trumpet players bucking each other, then the next night maybe saxes. The first time I went there it was a piano night.

There was James P. Johnson, Willie "The Lion" Smith, Fats Waller and some others. Well, as the night went on someone pointed out Duke Ellington to me. He never played all night but just sat there writing down music. Those guys were so "heavy" maybe he just didn't want to get on the piano. Who knows?

Duke was always hanging around Mexico's. In fact the first time that I played there, Luis Russell, bless his soul, told me, "We're going down there one night, and you are going to break them up." So he got me to rehearse *High Society*, which nobody had heard too much in New York. We rehearsed it like mad and when we got there we knew exactly what we were going to play. He started to put on. "Come on, Barney. Take out the horn and play something—anything," says Russell. So we played out *High Society* and broke up the joint. They all thought I was a hell of a clarinetist, but that was all I played all night: *High Society*. Duke must have heard that, I guess. He would come in and go out without much fanfare, because he wasn't like Willie "The Lion" and them, personality-wise.

It was the same deal when he came over to hear me at the Nest. I didn't even know he had been in there, or left for that matter. The night after he stopped by back came Braud once more. "Duke wants you to come over to his apartment in the morning to talk. He wants to see you. OK?" said Braud. That's how it all started.

Next morning I went over to where Duke was living. They used to have a theater in New York called "The Lafayette" and he lived just about two blocks from there near 7th Avenue and 128th Street. I wanted to hear what he had to say, so I punched the doorbell.

He came to the door and invited me in. We sat down and he came right to the point. "I want you to join my band," he says. "I don't know how long we're going to stay here, but we are trying to build up a good band. If we can do it, and the boss likes us, then we can stay at this Cotton Club a long time. We'll have a good job there." I noticed he kept talking in the plural: "Our band", "We can stay there," and liked that from the start about him. He thought of a band as a unit and I dug him.

We talked on for a half hour or so and he outlined his plans. He seemed to know what he was about to do and he made sense all the way around. I asked him about the hours and when we'd get off and how long we would play. Also about the money. It turned out to be a smaller salary than I was making at the Nest, but the more the man talked, the more I liked him. He was very ambitious, even then.

He told me that Irving Mills was booking him, and that Mills was also his publisher. He was "in" at the Cotton Club. You see, a lot of those Broadway show people used to hear Duke's band down on Broadway and they recommended him. That made it even bigger for him at the Cotton Club. I knew all those fine looking gals that worked there, because they used to come by the Nest after they finished work. They were some real beautiful babies, and that was another incentive right there. You know, the funny thing, he didn't even mention music at all that day. I mean, he knew that I could read, and from being with Russell he knew I could play too. He had heard it for himself. There was just something different about him from other people. For instance, I was much more impressed when Joe Oliver offered me a job than when Duke did, because Joe's band was so much better known, and yet Duke Ellington made you feel so much at ease. Just like he was going to turn the music business upside down and you would be part of it. Anyway, I told him I would join him right then and that I would give Russell my notice that same night. I remember he simply said, "Good. You won't be sorry. You can start next Friday." I started that Friday and ended fourteen years later. It must have been my best move in life, I think.

As far as I know, Duke had had his band for a few years before I met him. They mostly came from Washington. Originally there was Bubber Miley, Otto Hardwick, Tricky Sam or maybe someone before him, come to think of it, and Duke, Sonny Greer and a banjo player who they said was crooked. They kicked him out and made Duke the leader; then he hired Freddie Guy. That's what had happened before I joined them, as near as I can say.

Anyway, I went to my job at the Nest that night and told Luis Russell what had happened. He was such a great guy. He wasn't mad that I was giving notice or anything like that. He was just as glad to see me get such a good break. I guess he sensed that Duke would be going places. What made it even nicer was that when I told the boss I was leaving he said, "Well, son, if it doesn't work out, you can always come back. I'll be glad to take you back any time at all." That made me feel fine about everything.

That Friday I began work with Duke Ellington's Orchestra. The Cotton Club was a plush place. All the "biggies" would come there. They even had carpets on all the floors. It was a dining and dancing place mostly through the week, but on Sunday nights it was "Professionals' Night," meaning all the Broadway stars would come because there were no shows on Sundays on Broadway. There was no sign outside to advertise the band; it just read "Cotton Club." That was all. But the word went from mouth to mouth, and we had real big crowds there always. When I played my first job with the band, the personnel was Bubber Miley and Louis Metcalf on trumpets, Joe "Tricky Sam" Nanton on trombone, Otto Hardwick, Harry Carney and myself, and the rhythm section was Duke, Freddie Guy, Wellman Braud and Sonny Greer.

The band always lined up in the same way. Looking at the band from the dance floor, left to right, in the front was the trumpets, the piano was smack in the middle, then Otto Hardwick, me and Harry Carney. In back, on a raised up little platform, would be the trombone, the drums right behind the piano, then Wellman Braud with his bass, and Freddie Guy on guitar sat right back of me. We were there from nine in the evening to three in the morning, with intermissions on the hour. We played two shows each night to accompany the chorus line or acts that they had. These acts were great. I remember the Berry Brothers and the Nicholas Brothers got their start, dancing there with us. The first show would come on about eleven-thirty and the second show, a shorter one, came on around two-thirty. We played for dancing in between. Some of the acts brought in their own music, but Duke wrote for a lot of them.

I honestly can't tell much about my impression of the band that first night. I was too busy fighting the notes, the reading stuff, to pay much attention to the band. I remember the weird chords that would come in behind us. I wasn't used to that kind of chording at all, but the more I played with them, the more accustomed my ear got to it all. I used to go to Duke in the intermission and say, "Those chords behind me on such-and-such a number: they just don't sound right to me." He would sit right down and show me what he was doing. He'd break all the principles of arranging too. He'd give a guy different notes to what he should have had for his instrument. That was what he called "jungle music." Some new things were always coming out in that band. One night, for instance, Tricky Sam was sitting with his trombone across his lap for some head numbers in the last set. Otto Hardwick says to Duke, "Why don't you give that man a solo? He's all ready, but he's too bashful to ask you." "All right, Tricky," says Duke, "Off you go." I couldn't believe the sounds that he made on that horn with the plunger mute. I had never seen or heard the trombone played that way before, and my mouth was just opening and closing like, right along with him.

That set the whole band to laughing, but I was really amazed at the sound he came up with on that plunger.

When I joined, Duke had a "book" of his own with numbers like *Black Beauty* and *The Mooche, Birmingham Breakdown* and so on. That book kept getting bigger every day that passed. His theme song was *East St Louis Toodle-Oo* when I got into the band. As the nights went along, he and I both began settling down to each other's playing and he would write things around me. He would write a whole darned arrangement on a number of his own. He would leave out sixteen bars, say, and tell me, "OK. When you get to there, just take it." That was how he made you feel at ease. Like you belonged in there.

Duke was a real good leader from the start. I mean, for instance, he insisted that we all memorize the whole book so that when we started a song he would never knock off like Oliver and those older guys did. He would just start to play at the piano, maybe like a hint of the upcoming song, and then you would go for it. He never did the talking or public address stuff that he did in later years during the period I played at the Cotton Club with him. For instance, we broadcast a lot. I know that, but they had an announcer called Ted Husing and another one called Norman Brokenshire. They did all the talking on the air. Husing was a real fan of our band. He tickled me. When he introduced the members of the group and got to me, he would say, "And on the clarinet, my good friend, Barney *Byegard*."

A lot of people write how Duke always kept a disorganized band. I don't know where they got that crap from. I was there. I know. Maybe he had trouble with one guy or another, but he always got them out before any real trouble built up. It's funny, I never knew Duke to fire anyone. But I'll tell you, he was a slickster. He would make life so miserable on that job that you would just quit.

I think by comparison to Joe Oliver's band I found Duke to be a little less professional in the early days. Mainly because Oliver had a well-behaved band as well as being all good musicians. A couple of Duke's men were a bit on the wild side, but as time went by things fell into place better. As for the music, you couldn't kick on that. There was always something going on to keep your mind busy. At first, as I said, my mind was busy figuring out those strange chords that Duke kept putting behind me. It was so different to what I'd been used to in music. I figured out how not to get thrown though in those first months. See, Freddie Guy with his guitar, Wellman Braud on bass and Sonny Greer at the drums made the same rhythm as all the other bands I'd

Barney's mother, Emanuella Bigard

Courtesy DB

Barney's father, Alexander Bigard

Courtesy DB

i

Barney Bigard on the day he joined
Duke Ellington's band in December
1927

Courtesy DB

Sidney Bigard, Barney's brother

Courtesy DB

Joe "King" Oliver's American Federation of Musicians card for 1927 when Barney was in his band

The American Federation of Musicians card of Lorenzo Tio after he joined the New York Local 802 in 1930

King Oliver's Dixie Syncopators. Back row: Bert Cobb, Paul Barbarin, Joe Oliver, George Filhe, Bob Shoffner and Luis Russell (piano). Front row: Budd Scott, Darnell Howard, Albert Nicholas and Barney Bigard

Courtesy DB

iv

The Duke Ellington Orchestra during the Cotton Club period. Ellington at the piano with, clockwise round the piano, Freddie Jenkins, Cootie Williams, Sonny Greer, Arthur Whetsol, Juan Tizol, Wellman Braud, Harry Carney, Fred Guy, Barney Bigard, Joe "Tricky Sam" Nanton, Johnny Hodges

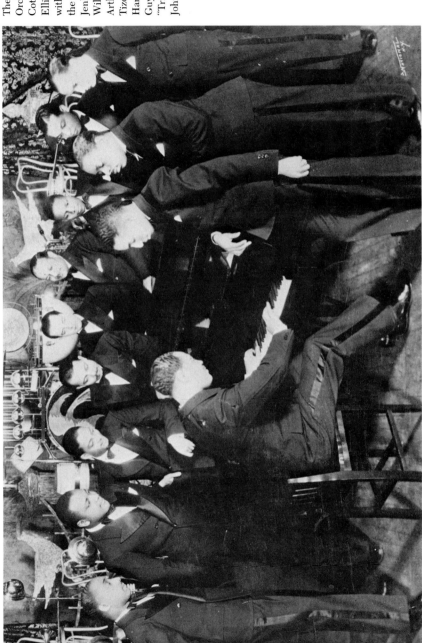

A period publicity shot
of the Duke Ellington
Orchestra

The Duke Ellington Orchestra at the time of the 1933 tour to England. Back row, left to right: Sonny Greer, Fred Guy, Wellman Braud, Duke Ellington. Middle row: Freddie Jenkins, Cootie Williams, Arthur Whetsol, Joe "Tricky Sam" Nanton, Juan Tizol, Lawrence Brown. Front: Otto Hardwick, Harry Carney, Johnny Hodges and Barney Bigard

The reed section of the Duke Ellington Orchestra: Barney Bigard (left, clarinet), Otto Hardwick (Center, standing, alto), Johnny Hodges (Center, crouching, soprano), Harry Carney (right, baritone)

been with. They played strictly four beats to the measure. But of course it would depend on the tune they were playing. Sometimes we would be playing something real slow like *Maori*, or another of those things. Then the rhythm section would go to playing two beats to the measure. But when it came to the all-night nitty-gritty, it was four all the way with that rhythm section.

Now, to get back to Duke and his weird chords. He would tell Freddie Guy the chord, but Freddie knew just one way to make a chord: the old way. Duke, he'd be experimenting with all kinds of different notes in there, but I didn't pay him any mind. I never listened to what Duke was making at the piano, but just listened to Freddie Guy all night. I took my stuff from his pattern, because that was what I was used to.

Duke was a funny man, though. You'd think he wouldn't be paying attention. Like, if you've got your part and you make what we call "skates"—in other words you play a bar different from what he had written—you'd think he didn't notice. He would just look straight at you and wouldn't say a word. Much later he would say, "You're not fooling me. Remember in bar so-and-so of such-and-such." Boy, he was something. With all he had on his mind he never strayed from the musical side of things. I mean, Irving Mills was the man who handled all of the band's business. We musicians never ever got involved. Mills would fix a deal and tell Duke, and then Duke would tell the band. There was never any doubt about who had the band though. We were working for Duke and not for Irving Mills. Mills had absolutely nothing to do with who Duke hired, and any difference between him and Mills was strictly between the two of them.

We were doing real good through those first months and things just kept getting better. We worked seven nights a week at the Cotton Club and very seldom had an off night. Duke lived up to everything he promised me, so I was happy. I mean, I was real happy.

The band was becoming much more of a drawing card than the location it played in. At first you could have put anyone in at the Cotton Club and the crowd would have gone along there, but now the band was gaining fans so fast that if we had moved to another place I think the people would have come along with us. From taking a drop in money, after leaving the Nest and joining Duke, I soon made a turn around. We did all kinds of broadcasts, recordings, and extra jobs in the mornings, or matinees. We went as far as to play in Flo Ziegfeld's *Show Girl*. Then we played a concert with a French guy called Maurice

Chevalier. We did the first half of the show and he did the second.
When he came on we went into the pit and played accompaniment to
his songs. He was all by himself out on the stage. He couldn't sing
worth beans, but he was a fascinating man to watch. He'd put that big
lip out there—"Louise"—and he sure charmed all those women right
out of their seats. It went so well that we held that job down for four
weeks.

Of course we still held forth at the Cotton Club with all of this extra
activity. That place was something else. I remember one night a little
guy came in with some blonde gal. He came around to the piano and
said, "Hey! Play *Singin' in the Rain*." Duke just nodded his head and
we played four or five more numbers and still no *Singin' in the Rain*.
He came up to Duke the second time and said, "I asked you for *Singin'
in the Rain*, goddammit! I'll grab you by your coat and choke the hell
out of you." Herman Stark, the manager of the Cotton Club, saw him
up there and came over and asked what was wrong. He knew Duke was
kind of stubborn, see. So this little guy says, "I asked him for *Singin'
in the Rain* and this son-of-a-bitch has played everything *but* that!"

"I'll get him to play it. You just sit down and cool off," says Stark. He
came back to Duke and said, "Don't you know who that guy is?" And
Duke says, "No, and I don't care who in hell he is either."

"That guy is Jerry Sullivan. He's the one been making all the news
for doing a stretch for Frenchie Dumaine, the gangster," said Stark.
Next thing you know, we were playing *Singin' in the Rain* for a whole
hour and it sounded mighty sweet to us too. You'd better not fool with
those gangsters in those days.

After that, this little guy got to be a big guy and later, when they
began kidnapping all those big-time show people for ransom, Jerry
Sullivan used to take Duke to work each night in his bullet proof car
with a machine gun between his legs. He'd wait the show out and bring
him back too. They got to be good buddies. Many years later we were
again playing Chicago and those gangsters wanted to give Duke the
"hot foot." He had upset them in some kind of way, so they wanted to
burn him, to make him limp a while. See, the gangs weren't making
much money out of bootlegging any more and they hadn't yet taken
over the numbers racket, so they tried to make their money by bearing
down on important people. They took it to the head man, Owney
Madden, and he called Capone. So Capone sent a couple of hoods
down to the theater one night, but Duke had connections through
Herman Stark and Stark talked with Capone and he called these goons

off. They burned Rudy Vallee and Bill "Bojangles" Robinson though. Seemed like Duke had better connections.

In spite of all these goings on we managed to concentrate on our music and our band. They didn't call 'em the "Roaring Twenties" for nothing.

When we started at the Cotton Club we wore tuxedos, but as we began to build up a band fund we bought other uniforms. We built that fund out of tips and added to it by fining each guy a dollar for every fifteen minutes that he came late to a rehearsal or band meeting. If you didn't show up at all and didn't notify Duke you weren't coming, then you forfeited a whole night's pay. That band was that strict. But to tell the truth, the money we used for new uniforms came mostly from tips. Like, guys would come in and tip us a hundred dollar bill. Things like that. We never had to put our hands in our pockets for uniforms or music and such.

Whatever good fortune smiles on a band, there is always someone or other that has to be Trouble. Ours came from Bubber Miley and Otto Hardwick. They were both real heavy drinkers, but I think Otto was the worst. He was a bad influence on Bubber and also on Tricky Sam, our trombonist. They would sometimes not show up and be off for days. Especially Otto. Bubber Miley would generally come back first and he would show up with his "dickey," which we used to wear instead of shirts with our tuxedos, all covered in "mess." He eventually figured out how to handle this situation, and he went out and bought a great big eraser. He spent most of the first set cleaning his dickey with this eraser that he left in his trumpet case when he went off on these binges. One thing, drunk or sober he could always play, and so could Tricky.

Otto Hardwick: we called him "Toby" and he was another deal altogether. He would be missing for two or three days. So one night I decided I'd go with him after we got off, just to see where he went all that time. Sure enough, I did go with him. Once—and only once. All that man did was go from apartment to apartment, friends to more friends, girls to more girls. And at each place he'd get to drinking something. I tried to keep up with him on that booze and, oh boy, I was dead for about a week with a bad, bad hangover. That's all he did: go visit all the people that he knew.

He would go his way, Bubber would go his, and Tricky would just go down to Mexico's, get stoned and sleep the night there, until he sobered up, and then come to work. Their drinking never hurt their music, but what bugged the rest of us was that every time some big-shot who could help the band would come down to the club, either one or two of them would be gone. Duke would get so mad that when they came back he would tell them, "Well, you all did a great job. We had some very important people in here to listen to you and you weren't here. That's great for the future of the band, isn't it!" Finally, he got so disgusted with them that he got rid of both of them by making life so unpleasant that they quit. After they went then Tricky forgot his bad ways and got into line again.

To replace those guys he got Cootie Williams on trumpet and Johnny Hodges on alto, and that's when Duke really began to build the band.

Things kept up at a hell of a pace for us all in Duke's band. They started to call it "Orchestra" after a while. Nothing changed but the name though. A few of the men maybe but the music and that money kept getting better and better. Sometime in the early 1930's Mills kept telling us about the demand for the orchestra all over the country. There was even some interest for us to go to Europe. I think we finally wound up at the Cotton Club in 1931. We went to touring and from then on until I left the band in 1942 it was eleven years of touring. We may have played for a couple of weeks in one place here and there but it was mostly traveling. We worked clean through the Depression without even knowing that there was one. I guess we were one of the best-paid, best-known bands in the USA.

I have read in jazz books that Duke's band was disorganized. That the guys never knew where they were going or what trains to catch and that their music was always missing. Stuff like that. I can tell you, all the time I was with Duke no such stuff happened. For instance we always had a full itinerary before we left New York. Mills would give them out. Everybody at all times knew what bus, train or boat to catch. They'd all be there too. We had a band boy named Richard B. Jones. He used to be a bus boy at the Cotton Club and when we left we took "Jonesy" with us. He was so loyal to Duke that later he became more of a bodyguard. He used to handle all the trunks. Put them on and off trains and bring them to the hotel to the rooms and all. He also kept the band's music and passed it out. Duke had the easiest band to handle in those years that he ever had. I mean the bunch he had much later, that was another world he had to be in.

NINE

"The fastest company in the whole wide world."

Johnny Hodges and Cootie were working with Chick Webb at the time Duke offered the job to them. They loved Chick so much and were so faithful to him that Duke had to practically get on his knees to get them to leave. Finally Chick himself told them to take the job because he was able to see that it would better them in the long run. He was just that kind of guy and he liked Duke a whole lot.

The way it worked from the inside of Duke's band, at that time at least, was like this. We would all get together to decide who would be best to hire as a replacement and then we all made our suggestions. After a while a decision was made and Duke would go to talk with the guy in question. That's how it was with Johnny Hodges. Harry Carney knew Johnny from Boston which was the home town of both of them. He suggested that we get Johnny into the band and practically everyone agreed that he was the man for the job.

I had always loved the way Johnny played. He was a striking individualist and always played with that beautiful tone. He got a better chance to express what he wanted to do with us than with Chick. I know for a fact that Chick had quite a few good soloists in his band but they played mostly ensembles. There were very few solos that the guys had. Mostly ensembles. When Johnny came with us then Duke pushed him out to the foreground. He actually came in before Cootie joined us.

Johnny was scared when he first joined us, I recall. I guess we all were at first because most of us had never before played with a large orchestra that was beginning to get somewhere. Naturally you get a funny feeling, and you're fighting to do good all the time until you can relax yourself. Its kind of a challenge and it scared Johnny plenty. He was a very quiet sort of a guy and everything that he would do would be done in a sincere manner. He and I became the biggest buddies. We'd pool our money and gamble and if one didn't win then the other would take what money was left and try. He was a load of fun, but you'd never guess because he always wore that serious face. Just like he was angry all the time. He wasn't mad or nothing, just shy. He was married at the time he joined the band, and had a baby. Later on he got a divorce from his first wife and married a girl in the Cotton Club show. They had a son somewhere along the line. He wasn't much of a drinker but he loved to play poker, to gamble. That's what we did all those traveling years. Of course we'd drink a little, but when I really started into drinking was later when Ben Webster came into the band. He'd do a lot of things that we wouldn't dare do and Duke would bawl us out. But he was afraid, I think, of Ben Webster. We saw that and we decided, "He lets Ben get away with it. We'll do those things. We'll get drinks ourselves." That's what caused me to start drinking heavy. But Johnny and I never did drink to such excess.

Hodges was really very interested in the music. Harry Carney and I would take him in hand and if Duke had written a new orchestration with a sax ensemble we would go over it with Johnny until he had it down pat. That was how he got to be such a good reader. I have never heard anyone play with that beautiful tone of his before or since. There will never be another Johnny Hodges. It was all his own style too. At first he was a disciple of Sidney Bechet, and not so many people heard him on soprano. He had all of those Bechet licks down, but then he developed that slurring, that tone of his own.

Johnny and I, we both liked exactly the same alto players in jazz. My all-time favorites were Hodges and Benny Carter. The other guy we both liked so much was Hilton Jefferson, that made that great record of *Willow Weep for Me* with Cab Calloway, I think. It's a great thing to be sitting alongside your all-time favorite in the same band every night, and that's just what it was like for me playing with Johnny Hodges.

Harry Carney was the other saxophone in the section with us. See I played half on clarinet and half on tenor, Johnny was alto and Harry played baritone. With those guys you were in the fastest company in the whole wide world and so I let the sax drop out bit by bit and devoted my entire time to the clarinet. Even now I don't care to play sax any more. But to get back to Harry Carney: he was four or five years younger than Johnny or I and had been with Duke before I had joined the band. Duke used to go all through the New England states and work for a guy named Cy Schribman. They were all-summer dates and Harry had played up there with Duke before me. Harry was a real swell guy, always trying to help out. I guess he worked in the band so long that it was more like his family. He knew just by his instinct just what the other guy was going to play and he'd match it. You just don't get musicians like that any more.

Working with Sonny Greer was a thrill too. He was a fantastic drummer. He was sharp, real sharp. A lot of times we'd be "fluffin'" and get off the music and Sonny would do some funny thing on the drums to save the band. He'd bring us right back in on time together. Sonny was never a great musician, technically speaking. In fact I didn't know of any of those drummers in those times that were very good musicians. Lionel Hampton should have been because he knew the vibes. But anyhow, Sonny Greer was just simply a good rhythm man. Like if he had a passage to play on chimes then Duke would mark off which chime to hit first and second. All that stuff.

In the band he would give us a solid four-four time. Whatever the specific arrangements called for. They might have a special lick in there in some places and Sonny had a keen memory. When we would play the thing down he had it all tucked into his head. He was on to it all, never miss. It was a powerful show we played at the club, but for the show or the dancers he was terrific. The only thing that bugged me about Sonny's playing was that you could be taking a solo and everything was going just nice, he would be giving just the right beat, and then someone he knew would walk in the place and he'd spy them and start to waving his arms to say hello. The beat would be gone right in the middle of your solo. But you couldn't get mad with him. That's just the way he was. Always friendly to people.

Cootie Williams was from Mobile, Alabama. He came up with Edmond Hall and they had some kind of band. When he joined us I think he had as much effect on the sound of the band as Johnny Hodges did, but naturally in a different way. He played his own way and in fact he was doing all that growl stuff before Bubber. I have read places that Duke tried to get him to sound just like Bubber. That's not true. That was Cootie's style. Just what he played with us in those days. Cootie was a big gambler too. Loved to gamble, and for much bigger stakes than Johnny Hodges and I could get into. When Cootie first came in he was alongside Louis Metcalf but then Metcalf soon left and Freddie Jenkins came in. We were also joined by Artie Whetsol on third trumpet and a trombone player called Harry White. Then White left the band and Juan Tizol came in. That was the best band that I can remember. Cootie, Jenkins and Whetsol, trumpets, Tricky Sam Nanton and Juan Tizol, trombones, Johnny Hodges, Harry Carney and me, reeds, Duke, Freddie Guy, guitar, Wellman Braud, bass and

Sonny Greer, drums. That would have been at the close of the twenties. Around 1929 I would say.

Wellman Braud was our bass man. He was the one that got me the job in the first place. He was a great guy, a wonderful man and also my other real good friend along with Johnny Hodges. We would always be playing tricks on one another in that band. But Braud and Duke they didn't get around to much of that. They were very "sober-faced" about all the goings on. Of course we couldn't do much to Duke with our pranks, but poor Braud. He used to play tuba. He couldn't really play the thing at all. He would just use brute force when he blew into it. No embouchure, just blow like mad. We got tired of that awful noise so we took a whole bucket of water and poured it into the bell of the horn before the show. Of course I had forgot that he used to stand behind me and sure enough when he started to wail on that tuba I got soaked.

Looking back we did some terrible things in that band. Like one of the guys would be trying to sleep it off before the job in the band room and we would sneak up and tie his shoe-laces together and we had a great big bell. We'd hit that bell and yell, "Fire! Fire!" and the poor guy, whoever it was, would jump up and fall all over his shoes, banging his head on the floor, with his hangover and all. Those guys would be so mad it would be way into the second set before they calmed down. We were like kids really with all that, but it seemed fun at the time. Of course Duke, he would have been up all night writing music and so he'd sleep through the intermissions in a corner somewhere. He never said anything about our crazy pranks.

Another time we put Limburger cheese and cayenne pepper on Freddie Jenkins' mouthpiece. He had a habit of leaving it on the stand before the show started, then putting it to his lips in the dressing room ten minutes before we hit. He jumped like mad. We took Artie Whetsol's valves all out of his trumpet and turned them around. Naturally his horn wouldn't work and he was there on the stand shaking it, and Duke just looking straight at him all the time. Like I said, Wellman Braud he was one of those real old-type of New Orleans guys that never really saw anything funny in this stuff. He was real serious, but he could play like hell on that bass violin.

The worst prankster of the whole bunch was Juan Tizol. You would never believe it if you met him casually. He always seemed so far above everything, but he was the ringleader of us pranksters. We used to play *Mood Indigo* and Tricky Sam, Artie Whetsol and I had to come right to the front of the stage for the three-part harmony on the first chorus. It was a real small stage and the curtain made it even smaller, so the three of us were real close up, and Tizol burst a stink bomb right behind us. They had those Klieg lights up full and they hit us full in the face. We had no idea of something thrown in back of us. Pretty soon I started to get a whiff of this thing. So I looked at Whetsol and Whetsol looked at me. I looked at Tricky and he began to giggle. This thing was getting stronger and stronger and the worse it got the more Tricky and I would be giggling. Arthur Whetsol was always the "prissy" one. Oh so sophisticated. He couldn't laugh if he saw a Charlie Chaplin movie. We had to give up for the laughing, Tricky and I, and went back to our chairs, but not Whetsol. He just kept playing as a solo. We said to Duke, "You ought to be ashamed of yourself letting something like that happen in your band." We figured that attack was the best means of defense.

After we came to find out it was Tizol—and we ought to have known right then and there—we fixed him. There was a novelty shop in the next block so we went out and bought some itching powder next day. We got to the dressing rooms early and put this stuff all in Tizol's tuxedo. All over his shirt. Everywhere. Hodges was in on it, in fact everyone in the band was in on it. I guess they had had enough of those pranks and seeing how he was the instigator we were going to give Tizol "holy hell."

We went up on the stage and the Klieg lights hit him. After half of the first number, and we were all watching him closely, the itching powder starts to work and Tizol starts moving around. When he started perspiring that made it even worse and after a few more choruses he was really going with that stuff. He couldn't make the end of the piece and had to run off the stage cussing everybody. He couldn't take it and it wasn't funny to him any more. That kind of broke him of that habit and the pranksters in the band cooled off now the ringleader was off it.

Tizol was no doubt the best musician in the band at that time. See, they all had a sound musical knowledge but Tizol could just transpose like mad. He could cover anybody's chair. All over the band, anywhere you put him in, he would go like mad. He was a terrific musician. I remember once we were making a record of *Conga Brava* and Tizol had a break. He break this break so it just sounded out of this world. It was great. A real gem, never-could-happen-twice sort of idea and it was so beautiful, but he stopped just short of the end and yelled, "Oh no. That's no good." Duke had a fit. "That was the best break you ever made in your life," said Duke. "Damn it. Why did you stop?"

"It wasn't perfect," said Tizol. He just wanted his music a certain way. Incidentally he never made the break again.

We had our set-backs in that band, naturally, but we won through the whole deal in the end. We had no real major catastrophes but I do recall one incident that almost closed us down the first week we opened at the Cotton Club. We had just started and the prima donna of the chorus line was a girl called Ada Ward. She and some of the other girls in the show had been dating the band that was in there before us. In fact that band had been fired and so the girls, especially Ada, wanted to get us in trouble so they would get rid of us and bring back the old band along with their boy friends. They gave us a real bad time and the boss Mr Stark told them, "Look. Stop trying to mess up the band, or something bad is bound to happen." So this main gal, Ada, would come out on the stage and sing a solo spot. She had insisted on a fiddle player to play obbligato for her, knowing we didn't use a violin. Duke had to go out and hire some guy. Anyways, before the show started this particular night, Otto Hardwick had sneaked in and soaped up this guy's bow, real good. After we played the fanfare, out she came and started that "Oooooh, Oh, Ooooooh, Oh" crap, and the guy that had the fiddle was sliding around all over the thing and there's nothing coming out. Oh, she was in another world by then and this poor son-of-a-bitch is sawing like mad. Still nothing. She finally ran off stage crying and complained to the boss. Mr Stark told her, "See. You should have let that band alone. I told you." After that we didn't have no more trouble. She was just as nice as she could be. Talk about polishing apples.

The audiences just loved the band at the Cotton Club and I remember that the most popular guys in the band seemed to be Hodges, Sonny Greer and Freddie Jenkins. The people were really rooting for them it seemed.

Irving Mills was always there. Every night. He and Duke were always cooking up some scheme for the band. Mills would tell the set up to Duke, and Duke would tell us what was going on. In those first two or three years there was plenty going on, believe me.

TEN

"They kept us runnin', night and day."

Irving Mills was the businessman. He would come up with so much work around town. Him and Duke they kept us runnin' night and day. I've seen times when Mills had us come to the studio at nine in the morning to make a record date, and we would sit there all that day and make nothing. Not even one record. It was just that Mills didn't like an idea, or something would have gone wrong. We didn't know or care the reasons. We got paid anyway for all the time we sat there. This happened not once but many times.

The first recording I made with the band was *Bugle Call Rag* and I remember that, for some reason, they couldn't use the drums. Of course Sonny Greer came there and sat through the whole deal, got paid and everything, but they just couldn't record the drums. Wellman Braud, bless his soul, he had to have the horn right close to his bass. He was coming over far too loud and they told him to move back some few feet. "Okay," says Braud, and don't you know he moved back sure enough, but be damned if he didn't take that horn right along with him. Everyone had their own individual horn see. After that we recorded for everybody. Sometimes under fictitious names. Duke was contracted for Victor but then we moved to Brunswick, then Columbia. I don't know how many records and stuff we made in those first years.

It was funny. If we had a record date to make next morning, Duke would bring a new arrangement on the job the night before, unless of course it was just one of our repertoire songs, and we'd rehearse it on the job because of that early morning date. If I had a part to play or a break to make then I'd stay up half the night trying to get it just so. And every time we would get into that studio I'd tense up and never make that thing like I had practiced it. I was so nervous about that horn or that mike standing right in front of me. Then it got so I said, "The hell with it. I'm not going to practice nothing. Just let whatever comes out come out," and don't you know those records began to sound a whole lot better to me after that.

I'm not bragging, because I don't even think about what I'm playing half the time, but like if people want to hear a certain tune I'll try to play it as close as I can to the melody. I'll go off on a tangent, probably, with my improvising but I try to keep that melody so they recognize it all the time. You can add little things, I mean whatever you want, but always let them know what they are hearing. That's the trouble today with all this bop stuff. Who in hell knows what's going on. Maybe the musicians and that's about all. I don't like all that monkey business where they are just showing off their techniques. That doesn't make music. Not to me. Use your "stuff" to good advantage.

But anyhow, we always had something going on. Matinees, extra jobs, recordings, and we even used to make motion pictures. I remember one with Mae West and another with Bing Crosby.

A lot of the guys were making records for Clarence Williams. He was some kind of early days A and R man. I wouldn't record for him because I was mad at him. When I had been down he would always get Buster Bailey and never hire me. I could have really used the money then too. Now he was always calling and trying to get me to record. I'm glad that I didn't because Red Allen had to fight to get the money out of Clarence. Red would go and knock on Williams's front door and Clarence would see who it was and go out the back way. Red got smart though. He jammed him. He'd knock at the front then run to the back and catch him.

It was around this time that I made records with Jelly Roll Morton. I remember the trio sides that we made very well. There was Jelly, myself and Zutty Singleton. We made these sides: something about a frog [*Turtle Twist*]. He always used Omer Simeon on practically all his record dates, but Omer was out of town when this trio thing came up. It had been on Jelly's mind to get those trio things off the ground and Victor went along with it. He was a big recording name for them and made a whole lot of money for them and for himself. The trio records must have sold really well because I remember I had to go to the Victor people to get copies. All the stores were sold out of them after that first week they came out and I couldn't buy one.

Jelly was kicks. He never was a bitter person right up until the end. He always loved to fuss and argue with somebody. He knew it all. He was a big shot at that time and could always talk a good fight. He and Chick Webb would stand on a street corner and argue so bad you could've become rich by selling tickets. Chick would just rile him to get him going. Jelly would tell Chick he was the greatest and Chick would tell him, "Yeah! Well come around to see my band tonight. We just got a new arrangement on so and so," and Chick would hum him the whole thing out of his head. Top to bottom. Jelly would say, "That ain't shit. Listen to this one," and he'd go to humming his stuff. People would all gather around. They thought there was a fight going on I guess. It was a show, those two guys. A whole show. Chick with his poor little crooked back and Jelly with that damned great diamond stuck in his teeth. I guess the ordinary people had never seen nothing like that before.

Anyway when we came to make those trio sides, we did it early one morning. We had a sketch of his tunes—a guide sheet in other words—and we went from there. He only gave Zutty and me the idea of what he wanted. He never told Zutty anything about the backing, but just let him feel it his own self. We ran over each piece a few times till we had it then we cut it. He didn't tell me anything either. It was his lead but my improvisations. He seemed pleased at the time with those sides. I know he was.

After those records I saw Jelly off and on and then he seemed like he was out of the picture for a few years or maybe I was just traveling so much. I saw him years later coming up 125th Street. He was all bundled up with his coat up high against the icy wind. "How's things going Jelly?" I asked him.

"Boy, those booking agents are smart people. They know if they hold Mr Jelly down, they can hold the rest of these cats down," he replied.

"Come on Jelly. That's not like you," I said.

"I'm getting ready to go to California," said Jelly Roll.

A few years after that I saw him again one more time. This time it was actually out in Los Angeles. He said, "I'm doing good out here. Got a place out in the country. Everything's all right. I'll make it." Next thing I heard, he had died.

ELEVEN

"Everybody in the band knew they were working with a genius."

Duke Ellington was one of the two geniuses I have ever worked with. That word is used so much nowadays; they call guys geniuses that I would have just called damned hard workers. But as to the real McCoy, I have only ever worked with two. The other was Louis Armstrong. They were both geniuses in different ways though. Duke is a composer and writer of ideas whereas Louis was a player of ideas. Louis could take any tune and make it interesting and beautiful and yet still you know that it's the tune. That's where his creative ability came from. Duke would actually write most of his own stuff. He would take an ordinary situation and put it into some music—orchestrate it—and before you could turn around there was a whole band orchestration based on some ordinary everyday occurrence. Like for instance *Harlem Air Shaft* or later his Sacred Mass stuff.

When I first met him I knew there was something different about him. Something that put him outside of other men. I couldn't figure out what he was doing with his music but I played it every night. I gradually got used to it and came to realize that he always knew exactly what he was doing. He never hit on things by luck; it was always in his plan musically. He came up with a different sound from all the other bands. Every time you would hear him on the radio you would know that it was his band. He had a distinctive touch to everything. He would take my clarinet part and make the trombone play it. He had the whole front section in different keys for some measures. Anything you like to name. But it was his music. The man and his music were one and the same after a while.

We were playing a concert for the New York School of Music and this professor of music had his class there. We were playing *Crescendo in Blue* and the professor had the class to figure out what Duke had done as a lesson. They couldn't grasp what Duke was up to and neither did their professor. Duke had to stand out in front of the class and go over what he had just played step by step. He had to explain it to the professor too. I remember that Gershwin wanted to collaborate with Duke once on an extended piece, but Duke turned him down. He thought it was "old hat."

Of course he was an open-minded man too. I mean if we would come up with a good suggestion, anyone in the band that is, he would generally take it. He would at least try it out. If you took a chorus and played a little piece of improvisation that he liked he would take it out and score it to make up a whole new tune. Then he would call a rehearsal. He would come there with maybe about sixteen bars. He would tell the guys, "Play this that's here, then Barney, or Tricky or whoever, you just ad lib from there." Open space completely. He'd figure out a chord structure to put behind it, then come up next day with a last chorus written out, and that would be how we'd record it later that same week. He could write around you. He knew your limits up and down and he would build the things around a given soloist's voice.

He would hear things and start to write even without a piano. That's where that number *Daybreak Express* came from. These southern engineers on the railroad, they used to have a fireman that would blow the whistle on the train. We'd all be up at night gambling and we'd hear the whistle blow as we went over a crossing. Duke would hear all the same things. The only difference was, we were playing poker and he was writing music about that whistling. He somehow got the effect of the train all into the music. He'd write all the ideas down and next day he would bring them to rehearsal all wrote out. You see Tizol was the extractor of Duke's ideas. Tizol had such beautiful handwriting. He would write all the individual parts out and give them back to Duke, who would in turn check them over then pass them out to the band.

Duke was a very patient man at rehearsals. Not like some bandleaders. Like if we were going to phrase a section part he would just sit quietly until whoever had the lead phrasing would get it down. Then the other men in that section would add their harmony parts or whatever. Duke would never get excited. He knew that it would all work out in the end.

The other thing writers all forget to mention is that Duke Ellington was a terrific band pianist too. He wasn't much on solos. In fact people would always be wanting him to come places to play and he told them directly, "Oh! I'm no good without the band." He genuinely meant it too. But like I said, as a band pianist he was just great. That is, once you got used to his chords. He would make the weirdest chords on practically any number. For instance if we played an old hat number like *Who's Sorry Now*, out would come those "funny" chords even for a number like that. I understand that he got a lot of his chord ideas from an old guy named Will Vodery that used to arrange for shows. He was the first Negro that went to Hollywood to arrange for a motion picture. He taught Duke a lot and Duke just kept on adding to it.

Another nice thing about Duke Ellington. He wasn't a surly kind of fellow in any way. He spent plenty of time with his fans, talking to them and giving them autographs. Most people don't know that side of him at all. All they know is the composer side. Of course that is what he spent the majority of his time doing. He wrote so much stuff you wouldn't believe it. Of course some of the guys in the band did contribute even without getting any credit. They didn't care about the credit; they were just musicians. Like Lawrence Brown had something to do with *Sophisticated Lady*, and Johnny Hodges had some part of *Don't Get Around Much Anymore*.

Duke and I had gotten together on *Mood Indigo*. I'll tell you what happened, just to set the record straight. My old teacher Lorenzo Tio had come to New York and he had a little slip of paper with some tunes and parts of tunes that he had written. There was one I liked and I asked him if I could borrow it. He was trying to interest me in recording one or two maybe. Anyway, I took it home and kept fooling around with it. It was just the second strain. There was no front part on what Tio gave me. I changed some of it around, for instance the bridge on the second strain, and got something together that mostly was my own but partly Tio's.

Duke had a date for a small group recording which in fact was supposed to be my group. We would record for all kinds of companies in those days and put the band under any kind of name with one of the sidemen signing in as leader. That was to avoid contractual complications. All the bands did it. Anyway, I brought what I had of the number to the date and we tried to work it out. We just used Tricky, Artie Whetsol and myself, along with the rhythm section. Duke figured out a first strain and I gave him some ideas for it too. He wrote out a three-part harmony for the horns, we added my second strain and recorded it. Whetsol had the lead, I had the second and Tricky Sam had the third. We didn't think anything of it and all of a sudden it began to get popular and that was it.

I missed the boat for twenty-eight years on royalties. I didn't get a dime. It was all under Ellington and Mills's name. You see in those days—just to show you how stupid we were—we would write a number and sell it to Mills for twenty-five or fifty dollars. If we had kept the numbers with our names on we would have had royalties for years and years. Now it has finally been legally cleared up for *Mood Indigo* and I do get my royalties from it. In fact I had an offer from a guy to sell the rights to it for $5000 plus 50% of any forthcoming royalty. I told him no. With any song you can register it every twenty-five years I think it is, then re-register it until seventy-five years are up then it's public domain. As you go along you get smarter and smarter but after you get taken a few times you know what is going on. Somebody that was doing a discography asked me why the number came out first as "Dreamy Blues." That was never the title. I always called it *Mood Indigo* but maybe the record company put the wrong label on the record. I never heard of "Dreamy Blues"; it was always *Mood Indigo* to me and I ought to know.

In the Duke Ellington Orchestra a lot of the music would be unrehearsed. Especially the soloing order. Duke would never have a set pattern, like clarinet then trumpet then bass or that sort of thing. After we played down his intro and main theme parts he had written for us then we would just take extended solos as we wanted. Duke himself would give us such great rhythmical backing at the piano. He knew how to "feed" somebody that's blowing a solo.

Duke only ever missed a job once to my knowledge. His mother had died and he had to bury her so he took off for a couple of days. They got Don Kirkpatrick, who was Johnny Hodges's brother-in-law, to take Duke's place. He did a fine job but the band wasn't the same. Everyone in that band knew they were working with a genius. Do you know till this day he has never had all the credit that he deserves. Like all other great artists. They have to be dead a hundred years before the world will really know their worth.

TWELVE

"The rigors of the never ending road."

It was the very early spring of 1931 when we left the Cotton Club and it was over eleven years till I once again could settle down and stay in one place. The world was now made up of theaters, trains, boats, hotel rooms, movie lots, radio stations, band buses which all come under the all encompassing heading "The rigors of the never ending road." Of course it wasn't a bad life once you took to it. Living out of a suitcase has its good points too, but you just don't have any roots. No place to really come home to. In fact home is with the band, year in and year out.

We played a couple of weeks at one time in some of the big theaters like The Palace on Broadway and 48th Street, or the Apollo and even the London Palladium but in all of my years these were the most confusing years. Your head stays in a permanent muddle because of the traveling. In fact all of the things happening here that I am telling are not in particular order; they just happened somewhere in the "road" years.

Like one time we were supposed to open at The Palace Theater in New York. If you played there, and went over big, then you had made it. It was like a testing ground for acts of all kinds. Anyway, we were all set to open and we had on our new white ties and tails, but most of the guys were real nervous because this was such a biggie. There was just two shows a day and if the public liked what you did, and you got those good first-edition notices, then you would work fifty-two weeks of a year automatically. This all being at stake we were shivering in the dressing room with apprehension. We knew all the critics and Broadway "big wigs" were out there. So anyway we took the stand behind the curtain. Then they pulled the curtain and we like to froze. Out came Duke and took his bow. He turned to us and waved the baton to get us to hit that great big chord that would start out our show. Down came that baton . . . nothing. Nobody moved or blew a note. Duke's eyes were blazing at us all but he turned and smiled sweetly to his audience just as if he were conducting for a "tea dance." He turned back to us, still smiling, and said in a loud voice, "Play you bastards." We got through that first week somehow and I'll never know how, but we got good press and we were on our way.

Another theater we played in Cleveland was a kick. Those poor people! We used to play *Black and Tan Fantasy* and while we were rehearsing the number I was just fooling around with the horn and grabbed high G. I flattened it, made a crescendo and held it out real long. Duke said "That's it. You keep that part in." So I practiced it up like mad till I could make it real good. So here we came with this thing on the stage. We got to my solo and I froze up. All that came out was a terrible squawk, then another and then a third one. The people just roared. They thought it was all in the act you know.

Then there was the time that Tricky Sam Nanton blew the back out of his trombone. Somewhere we were on stage and Tricky used to use first a trumpet mute packed tight into his bell, then a toilet plunger in front of that to get that "wa-wa" effect he was famous for. He came to the front to take his solo and he blew so damned hard that the tuning slide at the back end of the horn flew clean across the stage. He ran back and bent down to pick it up and that broke up the house. They just figured it was a comedy routine. What the devil. As long as they were satisfied.

Once we had a show somewhere out in the Midwest that they had us do a number with Jewish dialect. They wrote out all the words and everything. It started out with *The Song of the Volga Boatmen* and then had a little interlude and then the whole band was supposed to sing this chant. The people screamed, they didn't know what we were singing or trying to sing. We got all the words jammed up in there and everything. Maybe we were building a name for comedy too by this time. Those were crazy years, believe me.

I remember at one time during these years we came up against Jimmy Lunceford's band in Philadelphia. They were very popular at that time and had just taken on a new trumpet player called Sy Oliver. This Oliver guy, he didn't think much of our band and made no bones about it. The night of the "battle" Duke played all those funny-type tunes in the first set. When Lunceford went on this Sy Oliver character hollered, "Now we got 'em. We're going to fix 'em good." Cootie was real mad with Duke. "When are you going to play some of our fast music? This band is cutting us to pieces and you are playing all this crap," said Cootie. So finally Duke turned loose on them in the next set and we played like hell. The people all went to screaming and yelling and this guy Oliver was standing in the wings. At the end he came over and told us, "I just didn't know this band was so great. I take my hat off to you." After the show, Ivie Anderson, our vocalist, she liked to gamble. So she started gambling with Jimmie Lunceford's band and started winning all their money. That was the last straw, but it was fun for us.

During those days we made so many records. We even made those "Disc of the Week" things that was made of cardboard and sold for 15 cents. We made lots of movie shorts too. They still have them going around: kind of like a juke-box thing. We made one or two movie appearances too. That was the best deal because when you make a movie you get one fee for the recording and one for the appearance. We got paid by the week and the men were mostly all on different fees but all this additional work was paid extra so we were doing fine.

We did most of our traveling by train. We had two pullmans and a baggage car. They had sleepers and a diner. A couple of us got together and bought a little hot-plate stove and from then on we did our own cooking right on the train. We would have steaks or whatever we wanted. Duke soon got wise to our cooking and he put his money into the kitty and we cooked for him too from then on. When we got to the next town Jonesy our band boy would take our stuff over to the theater or ballroom. We'd play the job and right back on our train to the next gig. We never had any set program with the band; Duke just called the numbers like he wanted. From time to time a new guy would come into the band and Jonesy would just give him the "Book" of the guy he had just replaced. We didn't have too many personnel changes though. The rhythm section was always the same for years.

Around 1933 we had this offer to go to England. That was great because most of us had never been out of the States. A booking agent over there called Jack Hylton had contacted Mills about us making a trip. He had already booked Louis Armstrong and that had worked out good for him so now he wanted us. I guess they worked out the money to each other's liking and so we went. We got more money for being out of the country, I can remember. In the States or Canada we always got the same each week but this deal was better.

The first trip we made over there was by boat. I think it was called *The Champlain*. I enjoyed that boat trip a lot. We used to keep up our lip by playing in our cabins, but one night the whole band did play to entertain the voyagers. After that we had the whole boat to ourselves. We were welcome in any part of that big ship.

Once we arrived we opened at the London Palladium. We were the top attraction. That was a good gig, although we were so busy that we didn't get around much. We didn't even get a chance to meet many of the English musicians either. When we closed at the Palladium we played concerts around the country. I know we went to Liverpool, Birmingham and some place called Margate by the sea. Sometimes we went by bus and sometimes by train. Of course we were at home with the people because they spoke English, but we had a time trying to figure out what the Scottish people were talking about when we played Glasgow. They were crazy about our music and we got very good press. All too soon the trip ended and we came back to the States. We made three more trips to Europe later and I enjoyed every one of them.

When we got back to the States we had our first tour of the South. Duke didn't really want to go South because of the racial situation being what it was, but Mills convinced him. I guess he figured we couldn't come to much harm on those pullmans. We really didn't have too much trouble considering that we played in some of the worst Jim Crow places: towns like Shreveport, Louisiana, and Birmingham, Alabama. We played mostly dances but a couple of theaters. They would have what they called "split week" theaters then. Like three days in one and four in another. I mean Duke was a big name, even in the South, but they always had to have four cops stationed at each corner of the place so that the local people wouldn't get any ideas. When we played one town in the South that was supposed to be real bad we had some laughs. It was a real rough town. I can't remember the name, but anyway the cops would parade around the colored section because there was a ten o'clock curfew. You couldn't be downtown after ten or they would take you in and beat the hell out of you. We didn't know any better and we decided to walk back to the railroad station. There was about five of us and these cops stopped us and looked us over. One big cop looked us up and down and said, "Well. These niggers are different from the niggers down here." They just let us go on about our business.

After the trip down South we went out to California. I think that was when Lawrence Brown joined the band. I can't remember if it was before we went to Europe or after. We made two or three trips out to the West Coast. Anyway, on one of these trips we went out to Frank Sebastian's Cotton Club in Culver City, Los Angeles. Louis Armstrong was playing there as a featured artist with Les Hite's band. Duke really liked Lawrence's playing so he tried to hire him. We had trouble getting him to leave too. You see Lawrence had a brand new Cadillac that he just didn't want to leave. It was in storage and every day he'd go and wipe it off. He was just crazy about that car. He finally decided to take the offer and we had a hell of a trombone section. I loved the way he played. He was more of an executionist than Tricky Sam. He was more of a straight man, a great soloist. That gave us three different styles in the section: Tricky with all his growling effects, Tizol with that Puerto Rican stuff and Lawrence was the sweet man.

Lawrence was a nice guy but always squawking on something. He was never satisfied with anything. Always going to quit in five years. Like I said he played great and I loved him but he was just "grumpy."

So we kept traveling all through the middle thirties. The years just kept on traveling too. We went back into the Cotton Club a couple of times, then right back on that road again. One of the only good things about being on the road all the time was that you got to see plenty of other musicians and bands. It was a funny thing but there was so much competition going around that Duke really had to keep the band on its toes. I mean there were bands like Mal Hallet's or Woody Herman's and Artie Shaw's. All of them good too. The band that really copied us was Charlie Barnet's. If you heard them on the radio a lot of people would swear up and down that it was our band. The white bands were really getting going around that time too. The main difference in a white band and a colored band was that the white band would swing, but more politely. The colored musicians, as a rule, had jazz in their soul. The white boys, they just didn't have that feeling. Nowadays they are getting that feeling though. It all comes from ethnic groups if you ask me.

If you're poor you can realize more of something than if you are rich. By just being rich you don't have to bother about things so much. A lot of life just doesn't ever come your way. But if you're born poor, you feel it. That all comes out in your music. So many of the guys that suffered because of the racial situation and the economic situation in New Orleans for instance, they can't even read music, but they play with that feeling. That's all they have to offer.

White musicians also had a better schooling on their horns. The old white teachers wouldn't teach Negroes. I was lucky and had a first-rate teacher, but a lot of those guys didn't. You take guys like Benny Goodman, Artie Shaw and Woody Herman. They all play with feeling but they were taught right. Even from the start. It's easy to see how they made it, but now I'll tell you about one of the greatest instrumentalists that I ever heard in my life. This guy didn't have any knowledge about reading music but he became one of the most famous players in jazz. That's Sidney Bechet. The one and only—and I mean one and only—Sidney Bechet.

I first became acquainted with his music in New Orleans. He made a record of *Wild Cat Blues* with Clarence Williams I think it was. Everybody had that record. That was all you could hear. Every time you passed someone's house that had the door or windows open, they would be playing that song on their Victrola. When I came to New York that was when I actually met him.

Some people say Sidney was the most temperamental son-of-a-bitch in music. Others say he was the nicest man you ever met. I don't know. All I see is how a guy treats me and then I judge him on that. I didn't care what anyone said, he was strictly OK with me. See, there's no denying. He wanted a number played just like *he* wanted it, but even so he was always the one doing all the playing anyway. I don't blame him. He had to come up with all the fireworks so why not get the background like you want it?

Sidney was murder on trumpet players. Now he and Louis Armstrong couldn't get along so you know the rest of those horn blowers were going to catch hell. See Sidney and Louis were both "The King" on their instrument. They didn't record too much together because of the friction. One would want top billing and so forth and that would be a humbug right there, before they got to the music. They both wanted to play lead. Naturally if you're from New Orleans that's the old way. Trumpet always has the lead and everything else works round it. When they came to make those four sides together that's just about what Louis did. He played lead and kind of forced Sidney down. There was some kind of feud in there. I talked to Zutty Singleton one time about that session Sidney and Louis made and he says, "Man I don't want to talk about that session. Don't ask me nothing about it at all." All the time I played with Louis in later years he never once mentioned Sidney's name. Yet if they met on the street you'd swear they were madly in love with each other.

I can sympathize with those trumpet players that worked with Sidney. I mean what the hell were you going to play? He played lead all the while. I know him and Teddy Buckner got into it when they were at the Nice Festival some years back. Teddy told me about it. They were supposed to be making a record and Sidney says, "Put that horn down. You don't know what you're playing." I know that didn't please Teddy.

He was flabbergasted. I mean the man knows his horn upside down. On the other side, Sidney was up there as one of the all-time greats of jazz music. He played with so much feeling and that tone. Everyone loved what he played from the audience standpoint.

He had a lot of his own numbers too. He made one called *Petite Fleur* that sold a million. Funny thing was that it wasn't a biggie for him. Some English band went and had the hit with it. We went to New York right after Sidney died and they were trying to find out who his family was. I don't know if they ever found his wife but they had something like $300,000 waiting for her in royalties.

I guess Sidney started out with the clarinet but I know he used to fool around with oboe and bassoon a lot till he got with that soprano sax. That's what made him really to get well known and he never did go back to the clarinet. See, years before we went into the Cotton Club or before I was in Duke Ellington's Orchestra, Sidney was in Duke's band. They had six or seven pieces and Duke took them all up through the New England states. Even in later years Duke was crazy about Sidney. That sax part in Duke's *Daybreak Express* for instance. That's Sidney's part. Another one that was crazy about Sidney was Johnny Hodges. That was his idol, his early inspiration. Johnny used to take a few lessons from Sidney.

Maybe Duke would have kept Sidney in the band but he was always too hard to handle. Duke used to tell us stories about Sidney and so did Harry Carney. Harry was in the same sax section with Sidney in that early band of Duke's. Sidney Bechet was a real individualist but like so many guys he was unreliable. He would get stoned and just be lost for days. Naturally Duke couldn't put up with that. One time he was missing for three days and Duke asked him, "Man where the hell have you been?" Sidney says, "Oh I jumped in a cab and we got lost and I just now finally found out where I was." They was in that blasted cab for three days mind you! Sidney Bechet was one of a kind. In more ways that one too.

All those towns we played with Duke in the middle and late thirties gave us some heartaches and headaches but, like I said, we heard some great music. That was when I first heard Count Basie: in Kansas City. Now that was a band. Jesse Price was playing drums with them at the time I first heard them, Freddie Green and Walter Page were in the rhythm section and Lester Young was in there. They had this other boy that I really liked better than Lester. His name was Herschel Evans. Earle Warren was in the band too. That band had a whole lot of great reed men. Of course I liked Lester Young a lot when I heard him. He started a whole style. Now I really think the greatest tenor player in jazz was Coleman Hawkins, but I never could understand why he changed his style. I guess he tried to be like the kids coming up. From then on I didn't hear so much about Coleman.

The main thing I liked about Basie was that rhythm section. I think that was the greatest rhythm section there ever was. Like I said, Jesse Price was playing drums with them when we first heard them. He was a hell of a good drummer. Right after that they got Jo Jones in the group. But really that rhythm was different from Duke's or any band's. I mean with Duke we had Sonny Greer on drums. He was more of a show-off guy. He could give you a great beat when he wanted to, but Basie's rhythm was much more solid. Also, whereas Duke was a great band pianist, Basie, with his little "Ching-ching-chink" stuff, fitted in just right with his own band. The whole thing was one hundred per cent together, one hundred per cent of the time.

Duke himself loved Basie's band. He would go with us to hear them many times. In fact Duke and Basie seemed to get along real well. You understand, Duke was never jealous of anybody. He was just dedicated to music and loved to hear Basie play. Everyone liked the band. They started to get nationally known when John Hammond took a liking to them. To John Hammond there wasn't a band in the world like Duke's, until he heard Basie's. Then he got *Downbeat* magazine to build up Basie and then that became the *only* band to him, because he was personally behind it.

When we were in Kansas City, right down the street from our hotel they had another fine band: Andy Kirk and his Clouds of Joy. That's where we met Mary Lou Williams, the piano player. There was just so much music around in those days.

Sometime in the real late thirties we played St Louis with the band and I met another really great instrumentalist. They had a little after-hours place and Johnny Hodges, Ben Webster and I went down there to see what was going on. We heard this young kid playing the most string bass you ever heard in your whole life. It turned out that his name was Jimmy Blanton, he was around nineteen or twenty and he was working with Fate Marable on the boats. He was just stopping in to jam at this little after-hours joint.

Next night Johnny brought Duke down to listen to this kid and Duke was knocked out by what he heard. He asked the youngster to bring his bass over to the place we were working and play a number with the band. He came out on that stage and played the best *Body and Soul* you could imagine. Billy Taylor was playing bass with us at that time and he was flabbergasted. He just couldn't believe everything he was hearing. The things that boy was doing. He just started an innovation for bass players. He played the bass just like you would play a fiddle. He fingered the thing just like a violin but he had enormous hands and could really get around the instrument.

Duke asked him to join the band and so he did. We played for a while with Jimmy and Billy Taylor, but after a while Billy just up and quit. I loved playing with Jimmy. He was my very favorite among bass players. He was always practicing, practicing. Night and day. When he left St Louis to join us his professor gave him a list of all the symphony bassists in the towns around the country and a letter of introduction to them. Whatever we played, Jimmy would go look them up and go take his lesson. When the band played these theaters, just before we would be going on Jimmy was never to be found. Someone in the band got wise and went to look in the basement and there would be Jimmy practicing that bass. I remember one time a music professor in some city we played reviewed the concert and criticized Jimmy's playing. His original professor came to see the article and cut it out and wrote a reply to the newspaper saying, "If they only knew what that boy was doing, or if only they could find a way to do it themselves, they wouldn't criticize."

He gave incentive to all bass-fiddle players in America from then on. We made a record called *Jack the Bear* and Jimmy Blanton had all the front of the number just by himself. He started a whole new trend of bass players and from then on bassists began to get wise with copying what he was doing and all. With our band he played anything Duke wanted—two-four, four-four, six-eight—just anything at all. He was what I would call a "general practitioner" of the instrument. He was just as fast and accurate with the bow as the fingering. On top of that he was just so studious. The girls loved him, he just attracted them in droves. But he would just laugh them off. They'd find out the hotel he was staying in and they would call his room. He'd answer and say, "Yes. Just a minute. I've just got to finish what I was doing." Don't you know he would just leave that receiver down and forget they were on the line. Just go right back to that bass and start in with his practicing again.

He stayed with the band only for a short two or three years and while we were playing in Los Angeles he took very sick. They rushed him to the hospital and they found out that he had tuberculosis. They kept him in that hospital and I hadn't seen him in a while then one day I went over there to see him. He was lying in the bed laughing and talking and he was supposed to be getting better, but then they told him that he couldn't play his bass any more and he kind of lost the will to live. He died aged twenty-four and left behind him a whole legacy of ideas. I hated to see him die because he never got to fulfil his potential. He was the greatest bass player in the world.

To jump back a bit, there were two things that came into my life that changed it a good deal. First, there was the war in Europe and later the world. I had never seen anything like the change that World War II brought about in the world. The whole of life as we knew it was to change and in pretty quick time too. We were in Europe on tour with the band. In fact we were in Holland just when Germany was fixing to invade the place. We were supposed to carry on through to France playing concerts. They canceled part of the tour because of the ruckus that was just about to start and I know that we had to "high tail" it back to England and get out of there fast. As we were going across Holland we could see out of the train windows that they were putting machine-gun posts in all the haystacks and in the ditches. It was kind of scary I can tell you. Eventually we got to England and caught a boat back to New York. I was never so glad to see that old Statue of Liberty. Luckily it was to be another year or more before we got into it. Of course we would read all about what was going on in Europe in the papers, but for us we had a reasonably easy time back on the road.

Sometime after we got out on the road in the US again we played Pittsburgh, Pennsylvania, and that's where we picked up Billy Strayhorn. He came in and had an interview with Duke. They took a liking to one another and each other's work and finally, when Duke had discovered how great he was, they got a deal together. Then Billy became more or less our permanent outside arranger. He and Duke put some great stuff together for the band. One of the really good things we were involved in around that time was the show *Jump For Joy*. It was a musical that Duke and Billy wrote the whole score for. There were some acts and they were interspersed between the music. Acts like "Pot, Pan and Skillet," that kind of stuff. The show opened in Los Angeles, then it was supposed to play San Francisco, Chicago, Boston all the way across the country to wind up in New York. The backers got chicken-hearted and took out their money. That ended the thing and it was a shame because a lot of money could have been made out of that show. That was towards the end of the summer of 1941.

The second thing that happened to change my life was not until the last part of that eventful year. It was an eventful one because in that same month the US went to war right after Pearl Harbor, and I met my second wife Dorothe.

We were playing the Orpheum Theater in Los Angeles and I was living in a nearby hotel. I walked into a bar near the theater one night and saw a woman sitting with a crowd of people. She was wearing a great big red hat. One of the crowd of people was an acquaintance of mine who worked in the union called Elmer Fain. I asked him who this woman was and told him to tell her that I'd like to meet her. We were introduced and had a short conversation and I tried to date her right there and then, but "no soap." Anyway I gave her the number for the backstage theater and asked her to call me. She said she would.

Every day I was expecting a call but none came. No call. Nothing. I had about given up on her when one day, right out of a clear blue sky, I was called to the phone and she was on the line. We made a date for that same night and she said she would pick me up after the show in her car. When she arrived she had this little bitty car. It turned out to be her brother's. We went out someplace and had a couple of drinks and talked for a long while. I was still trying to get somewhere, you know. She told me right out, "I don't stay out with nobody that I have only just met." That made me kind of angry and I thought, "Well that's the end of it." But no! She came back for more. Just wanted to see what made me tick I guess. We got to seeing a lot of each other. It didn't seem to mean a whole lot to her that I was with Duke's band. She didn't even like the band much anyhow—she was a Benny Goodman fan— but she did start to dig us when she came to the show and saw us live.

Of course the job ended and I had to go back on the road. Naturally she had her family in Los Angeles although she was actually born in Wyoming. We wrote so many letters across country I guess the mail man got tired out from delivering. They had a record going around at that time by Tommy Dorsey: *I'll never smile again, until I smile with you*. That became our "torch song." Finally one day we were in Virginia Beach on the East Coast and it dawned on me where it was all going to wind up. A little later we were married.

Meantime things were getting rough with the band on account of the war. It was nothing like the things people had to contend with in Europe by all accounts, but it was still pretty bad for the average

American, let alone a traveling musician. We used to have to take such bad accommodations on account they took the pullmans away for the war effort. We traveled on the regular trains and it seemed like the whole country was on the move to someplace or another. The trains were always packed and jammed and lots of times we had to sit in the aisles. It was getting to be a drag. I had been on the road with the Duke Ellington Orchestra almost non-stop for almost fourteen years but this was not my idea of having a good time.

I had some offers to leave Duke through the years but I never cared for them seriously, but around early 1942 I had an offer to join another band. So did Johnny Hodges, and I figured that I wouldn't be so happy if Johnny went. Anyway I hung in there for the present, but it seemed that things got worse by the day. It wasn't anything like the way things went down for Joe Oliver years before. I mean we were still getting the same salary with Duke, war or no war. It was just that after all those years on the road the smallest things get to you. Silly things like sleeping bad, eating bad, traveling in crowded trains, couldn't get cabs when you needed them. All that stuff.

So when we got somewhere near California I made up my mind to give Duke my notice. When I told him I was leaving he just looked at me and didn't say a word. I have often wondered what he thought that night. After all, fourteen years together through thick and thin was a chunk of his life, as well as mine. My notice terminated at The Trianon Ballroom, Los Angeles, in June 1942 and I left Duke Ellington's great orchestra. I just wanted to rest for a while. Of course the papers played up the thing with all the wrong angles and made like it was the biggest thing since chopped liver. I never knew why the big deal. Maybe they thought that I would go back to Duke. That was out. Once I make up my mind I don't ever go back and change it.

Quoted from *Downbeat* magazine Vol. 1 No. 2 July 1942

As reported in this column, Barney Bigard plans to set himself up in business in New York. Barney hails from New Orleans and has been featured with Duke Ellington for years. Duke hopes to replace Bigard with another famous Crescent City clarinetist, Ed Hall, currently appearing at the Downtown Cafe Society with Teddy Wilson. Hall refused the offer, and Wilson, possibly in retaliation, offered Johnny Hodges a job at the cafe. All these dickerings may prove to be a bombshell as Hodges may accept. This may mean that four of Ellington's ace sidemen are leaving. Ben Webster has already left and Harry Carney may enter the armed forces any day. Let's hope this isn't the case, because Ellington's great Orchestra should be kept intact at all costs.

PART TWO

PART TWO

THIRTEEN

"The guys all asked me what I wanted with that old man."

Somehow it seems that what ever you plan in life turns out a different way. Maybe it was in the cards, but I quit Duke's band in Los Angeles and my wife was from there. I loved the climate and so we decided to make LA our permanent home. Dottie took a job at Northrup Aircraft and I had some money saved. I was tired of playing clarinet every night and of traveling and I just wanted to rest from it all for a while to see how things would work out. I didn't have to wait long to find out.

About a month after I settled down in California I had a call from a guy that wanted me to get a band together and play his night club. The guy's name was Billy Berg and his club was called the "Capri" on Pico Boulevard. He was a fantastic man. He loved music and he would take a chance on anything. He brought Dizzy Gillespie out to the Coast in later years when nobody was interested and he helped so many musicians get a start in Los Angeles. Guys like Eddie Heywood, Louis Jordan, Slim and Slam, Nellie Lutcher, and, believe me, she is something else, Nellie. Great entertainer. He promoted anything that he personally liked and he had a great staff working for him at the Capri. He died years ago, bless his soul, but the music business owed Billy Berg a great deal.

Anyway, I went down to talk over the deal of my band with him and he told me to get together a band under the name of "Barney Bigard's All Stars" and he would give us six to eight weeks straight. I told him that I would need time to rehearse it and get some material together so he suggested I come to work right away and rehearse my band in the day-time. So while I was rehearsing my band he put me to work at his club playing with Teddy Bunn, Leo Watson and the Daniel brothers. I played there with that bunch as a "single" for about a month while I was getting my group organized.

I hired me a trumpet player called Red Mack and a great bassist called Charles Mingus and a piano and drummer whose names escape

me. We opened about a month later and did good business right from
the start. We packed the place from nine till two most every night. The
band got very tight working there. I really liked the way Charlie
Mingus played. He was a disciple of Jimmy Blanton and Jimmy was my
all-time favorite. There was a little dance floor at the Capri and tables
all over the rest of the floor.

It was right around this time that I met a real old friend. Talk about a
"ghost from the past!" Who should I bump into one day but Edward
"Kid" Ory. Of course we knew each other from my childhood, when
my uncle Emile led Ory's band. The depression had hit Ory hard and
he looked a whole lot different. He told me he had been out of the
music business for a long while and hadn't played a job in years. Some
of his old band were living out here too. Tom "Papa Mutt" Carey, Ed
Garland, Bud Scott. All "home-town boys." Ory told me that he had
been working as a cook for a while but when I met him again in 1942 he
was sweeping out the city morgue for $12 a week. I hated to see the old
man in such bad shape so I asked him to bring his horn over to the Capri
one night and play a bit with my band. He wasn't too keen at first but I
kept after him and finally one night he showed up with his trombone.

Now here's where I want to set the history books straight. I have read
a hundred times that Ory joined my band on bass. I don't know where
that story came from but ask yourself this. What would I want Ory to
play bass for when I had one of the best bass players in the country in
the band already? Ory never did play bass with us. He came out there
that night with the trombone and that's how it stayed.

So this night he came out and he stumbled through a couple of his old
compositions, *Muskrat Ramble* and *Ory's Creole Trombone*. When he
played the little spot he just broke it up. The people came all around
the bandstand to see him. I mean this guy was a museum piece to them.
Most people thought he was dead, let alone still able to play his
trombone. The guys all asked me what I wanted with that old man but I
just told them, "Look. Can you make that audience break up like he
does? Don't worry. He'll bring plenty of customers in this place." He
did too. We never advertised him being there except for little cards on
the tables. That was the only thing bearing his name, but nevertheless
he pulled people in every night.

Ory and I got to be even better friends socially. He would go
crawfishing with me when the season came. He was like an uncle to me
through those months but later on he seemed to change completely.
But at this time we were buddies. He and his brother John were in

some kind of partnership. Ory lived on 33rd and Central and his brother lived on 37th Street. John had this huge back yard where they were raising chickens and a few turkeys. I don't know who was dumber: Ory or the turkeys. When I went out there first, these stupid turkeys wouldn't eat and so Ory had to put some little chicks in there to show them how to eat. Ory wasn't far behind them. If one of these turkeys caught a cold here he would come with the big cylindrical thing and shove Vick's Nasal Spray up their nostrils. Getting around Thanksgiving he would get lots of orders for these birds but there was one great big one he said he was going to keep for him and his brother. So come Thanksgiving Day they had sold all the turkeys save for this big one and when they came to get him, he had died. He swallowed a pebble and couldn't get it through. They had to go out and buy a turkey to put on the table. Boy! That was something. They had that business for a good while, Ory and his brother John, but then the brother took with a heart attack and died and Ory disposed of the place.

I kept telling Ory to get his band together. I mean most of the guys he used to work with were out here in LA to begin with. I don't know why Ory didn't see for himself that that would be the right way to go. I guess he just thought that his days were over and that he wouldn't be able to get any work with a band of his own. Anyway he was working regular with me at the Capri, but then fate took a hand in both our careers and he was pushed into going for a band of his own.

Fate for me came in the form of an offer to join Freddie Slack's Band. Freddie was a very good boogie pianist who played on the order of Meade Lux Lewis and Jimmy Yancey. He was originally the pianist with Jimmy Dorsey but then he got his own band together. He was the guy that made Ella May Morse popular. When I joined him he had a big band of fifteen or sixteen pieces that he would direct from the piano. I got to do all kind of work with his outfit. I mean it seemed like we were making a movie almost every month and then we'd play dances up and down California every weekend. Sometimes we would be in San Diego then the next weekend maybe San Francisco, all up and down the Golden State.

Freddie really could play that boogie stuff. He would practice all the time but he used to drink an awful lot and that's what hurt him most. He was the sweetest guy in the world when he was straight, but when that liquor got him it was like Dr Jekyll and Mr Hyde. After a while he lost all his contacts in the studio on account of his drinking. He was quite a guy, though, when I was with him—God bless his soul. If I wanted a raise I would go to him and say, "Freddie. I just can't make it on what I'm getting. How about you giving me a raise?" He'd say, "Oh! You don't want no raise," and he'd take me around town and we might pass a haberdashery or a suit store and we'd be looking in the window, then he'd start. "Look at that beautiful suit. Let's me and you go in there and look at it." First thing you knew he'd take me in there and have the guy find my size and he'd buy it for me. He would never give me a raise but he would buy anything for me, to keep me happy. He was just that type of a guy and he knew that I couldn't get angry with him. He was too good to me.

The only thing was that apart from me and a couple of others, his band was always changing. He had mostly studio men in there. Guys like Howard Rumsey, Les Baxter, Charlie Grifford, Davey Coleman, Ralph Lee and a singer called Margaret Whiting. Being all studio men they were all such good readers that they could come and go and the sound of the band wouldn't change too drastically. We never got the sound together too well though, to my idea, on account of all the changes. I stayed with Freddie the longest of any of them and even after I quit and he went to Chicago he would always call me long distance. "C'mon Barney. C'mon out here and join the band again," he'd say. I'd tell him, "No Freddie. I just can't make it."

"Oh! You don't love me any more," he used to reply.

"Yeh! I still love you, but I just can't make it."

He was a real sweet guy to work for and I enjoyed every minute, but what caused me to quit was that I had a good offer to go into the Onyx Club on 52nd Street in New York. This contract was for twelve weeks, and so I took the offer.

Actually, I went to New York because I won the Esquire All American Award for 1944 and, incidentally, for the following two years also. They told me that I had won the silver "Esky" and would I come to New York to collect it. It was something like the Oscar celebrations. I had won the silver for clarinet and Benny Goodman had won the gold. In fact there is a photo somewhere that we had taken with the saxophone winners too. All of the winners of the awards came to New York to collect them because it was a real great honor. They asked us to play a poll-winners' concert at the Metropolitan Opera House. I was too glad to play because of the company. Some of the real big people of American jazz. It was while I was in New York that I got the offer to take my own band into the Onyx Club.

I hired Joe Thomas on trumpet, Cyril Haynes (I used to call him "cereal oatmeal Haynes") on piano, Billy Taylor Jr, bass and Stan Levy on drums. We had a nice little group in there. We had some arrangements done for the band. Numbers like, *Little Coquette* and stuff like that. They were real tight arrangements mostly built on a counter melody in each case. Anyway, the people enjoyed us and we stayed out our contract.

Meantime, Ory and I had been keeping up correspondence and he told me that he had put together his old band, or at least most of them. When my New York deal came to an end I went back home to Los Angeles and saw for myself what Ory was up to.

Orson Welles was in Los Angeles. He had gained world-wide fame for his two pictures *Citizen Kane* and *The Magnificent Ambersons* and was now running a series of broadcasts called the "Mercury Theater Broadcasts" over CBS. He was also working on the filming of *Jane Eyre* at the same time. Apparently Welles had asked Marili Morden of the Jazzman Record Shop if she could locate a real authentic New Orleans jazz band for a broadcast in March of 1944. She turned to Ory who put together a band with Mutt Carey, trumpet, himself, trombone, Buster Wilson, piano, Bud Scott, guitar, Ed Garland, bass and Zutty Singleton on drums. Zutty was the only one that was working on a regular job at the time. He was a "biggie" around Los Angeles. They didn't know who to use on clarinet and someone suggested Jimmie Noone. He too had a regular job working with his own quartet at a place called "The Café de Paris" on Hollywood Boulevard. They had the band downstairs I remember.

Anyhow they made that broadcast in March of 1944 and they were so well liked that the people all wrote in and called in to say they ought to put the band on again. It was really through that broadcast that Ory got his comeback started. Altogether they played four broadcasts and then Jimmie Noone dropped dead. Because they were in such a rush with the confusion of Jimmie going just like that they hired Wade Whaley to play the next week's broadcast. He was so horrible that they let him go after one date and contacted me about doing the rest of the shows. I guess it looked to Ory like an indefinite contract because they were really popular and Orson Welles had a long-term contract. So the CBS people called me and asked would I continue on with the weekly broadcasts. I asked what they was paying and they said, "Scale." I told them no, flat out no. So they asked me what did I want to do it. I told them I would do it for a $100 a show and a short-term contract that I would get paid every week, play or not. They said they would talk it

over with Mr Welles and get back to me. A couple of hours later they
called back to say the deal was on, and I started with Ory's band for
those broadcasts that May.

The following week, for some reason, they didn't use the group. I
didn't care but my deal was for a $100 play or don't play. They never
sent my money so I went down there and argued it out with the
contractor. He gave me a load of bull and when they wanted us to play
the following week I told them, only if I got the money from last week
first. So, to cut a long story short, they paid me for the week I didn't
work too, but the contractor told me not to tell Ory and the rest of the
band. That was the very first thing I did do because they should have
gotten money too. I told Ory, "Look. You and your men ought to have
got paid for last week," and I showed them the check. They didn't do a
damned thing. Wouldn't even open their mouths. Mind you I don't
suppose any of this went on with Orson Welles' knowledge because he
was a real swell fellow. He loved jazz and had a great knowledge of it.
We used to go up to his house after the broadcasts and he would tell me
things about my career that I had forgotten myself.

Somewhere after the broadcasts ended Ory made some commercial
recordings with the same bunch of guys except that Zutty had left and
Alton Redd was with them. They were made for this Marili Morden,
who was then married to Neshui Ertegun and somehow they had
gotten Omer Simeon to take the day off from Jimmy Lunceford's band
to play clarinet on those sides. Meantime Ory had landed a little job
with a quartet at a place called the "Tip Toe Inn" on Whittier
Boulevard. He was using some guy from Oklahoma on trumpet, Buster
Wilson and Alton Redd. That's where Joe Darensbourg used to go and
sit in with them on clarinet. Joe always was a good player and Ory had a
chance to take his band into the "Jade Room" on Hollywood Boulevard,
so he hired him on clarinet. He got Mutt Carey and Garland and Minor
Hall and Bud Scott and started that job and that was that. His second
career was just beginning.

FOURTEEN

"I never was conscious that there was a whole movement."

The history books on jazz tell you that with the happenings out here with Ory's band, coupled with Bunk Johnson and George Lewis and their thing in New Orleans, there was a whole revival movement sweeping the country. I never was conscious that there was a whole movement going on. In fact I was too busy working to pay any attention to anything. I guess, to be truthful, that there was a lot of New Orleans dixieland players working that couldn't find a job for years. Some people were trying to build them up and generally succeeding. I mean there was a woman out here named Marili Morden that helped Ory get some jobs. She was once married to Dave Stuart, who was one of the guys that rediscovered and recorded Bunk Johnson. Then a little later she was married to Neshui Ertegun. They had a little record store on Santa Monica Boulevard in Hollywood called the "Jazzman Record Shop." Later Neshui went on to own Atlantic Records, but in the mid 1940s they had a small record label called Jazzman or Crescent. One of the two.

Joe Darensbourg had come down to Los Angeles from Seattle and I think he got the recording date for the Exner label. Anyways, this Doc Exner guy came down to LA and recorded the band. This was their second commercial recording session. A little later, Marili Morden recorded the band again but instead of Joe, who was the regular clarinet player in the band, they used Omer Simeon who was on the first records. See Omer never was regular with Ory's band; he just made the records. Joe Darensbourg was their clarinetist for most of their early years. Then he left and Darnell Howard joined them. After that came a whole string of clarinet players.

A whole lot of people think that I was with Ory's band around these years. That just wasn't so. I never joined Ory at all. Of course I made records with him. I made those broadcasts, but always as an independent contractor. Really it was more to help Ory. He and his wife,

Elizabeth (we called her "Dort") were as close as to be almost family. The old man was like an uncle to me. We made a whole set of records for Columbia with Ory's band. I hadn't played that kind of music for years and years but the records came out fine. Even I was surprised. I guess by being from New Orleans helped me a whole lot. I mean I never had to learn the songs or the style. It was the same old stuff I had heard and played when I was coming up. I liked the free style with no arrangements. It was different after all the bands that I had played with for the past twenty years. I honestly feel that in order to play good dixieland you must stay away from heavy arrangements. I still feel that you can use "head" arrangements, like talking it out and deciding what to play before you start, but that's a whole different thing to sitting there and looking at the notes. With those heavy arrangements you are not free to express your feelings; you are just too busy fighting the damned notes.

Over the years a lot of jazz fans have asked me what I thought of the bands involved in that New Orleans revival of the 1940s. Like I said, I was really too busy to think anything about them. I never knew Bunk Johnson or George Lewis. Bunk, well, he was pathetic to begin with. People just capitalised on him. They took him out of the country and bought him new teeth. He was doing alright until he began to start getting drunk and missing concerts. Things like that. He went around telling people that he taught Louis Armstrong, and Louis, bless his soul, he was so good about the whole thing that he wouldn't let you know any different. But he knew Bunk didn't teach him anything. I mean Bunk never could play like Louis in his life or like Buddy Petit, and Petit was Louis' big influence. I heard Bunk play in a concert up in Chicago and he was sad. No technique, nothing. There were guys that come out of New Orleans that played so much more horn than Bunk. I mean like Punch Miller. Even old guys like Chris Kelly played more than Bunk. I used to hear my uncle Emile talk about Bunk but I'd never heard anything sensational about him. Sidney Bechet had a short-lived band with him and he wouldn't take any of his crap. One time Bunk made like he was the big shit at one of Louis Armstrong's concerts and Louis even told him off. A lot of those old characters from New Orleans think that anything they do is alright just because they come from New Orleans. They think they can walk on your head if they want, but it just isn't that way.

In the same way I never heard of George Lewis. I heard him play once at the Beverley Cavern and once again when Louis Armstrong and I went to see him in New York. This time in New York he was so sick he couldn't play at all. I heard he was a nice enough guy but as to being the legend that people built him into? Willie Humphrey was more of a legend than George Lewis. A lot of those New Orleans guys bullshit about who they played with, but Willie always was with good bands and was always a real good musician too. I have read in articles that such a one from New Orleans played with Duke's band for two months or that another one played with Duke for three weeks or whatever. Now you take a lot of people. If you get popular they will come out and say, "Oh! I knew him way back. I played with him." All that stuff. Like maybe a guy will come and sit in one night for two numbers and next thing he'll be claiming that he played with you for ten years.

Another band that was somebody's idea of greatness was playing out here around this period. They were called the "Yerba Buena Jazz Band." Lu Watters and Turk Murphy had the band I think. I never cared for their kind of music at all. I hate to say it but in that style it seems that everyone plays out of key. I mean the clarinet player I heard with them seemed to know his horn but was so out of tune the whole time. What kind of ears do they have? He must hear that he is out of tune. I don't like that kind of rhythm either. They pull the rhythm down to me.

But to get back to Ory. I made a picture with his band too. It was called *Crossfire* and starred Robert Young, Robert Mitchum and Robert Ryan. I don't remember too much about it but I do remember Bud Scott had to sing *Shine* in that old deep voice of his. The band wasn't seen on the screen but just played some music behind some of the scenes. I made some music for another film called *I Dood It* with Red Skelton. That wasn't Ory's band, just a studio-type gig.

Like I said before, Ory and I would go catching crawfish together a whole load of times, then we would go back to his house and clean them and cook 'em. One day we were sitting in his house preparing these crawdads when out of a clear blue sky I asked him, "How much royalties do you get out of *Muskrat Ramble*?" I don't even know why I asked. I guess more out of conversation than curiosity. "I don't get nothing," came his reply and I almost fell off the chair. He said he never sold it to anyone since he had composed it that day for the Louis Armstrong Hot Five recording. That was some twenty years before and it had become one of the all-time dixieland hits in the meantime.

His publisher years ago had been Melrose Publishing Company and they had sold the song to another publishing company and Ory had never gotten "nickel one" from the song. I had some friends in the music publishing business on Vine Street in Hollywood so I called and asked them who published *Muskrat Ramble*. These friends looked it up and said that the Levy company had it. I took Ory down to this Levy Publishing next day. They were on the second floor of a big office block. We got there and the secretary said that Mr Levy was in and for us to wait a moment. "Who shall I say wants him," she asked. "Just tell him Barney Bigard," I said. I didn't want to mention Ory just yet. We waited a few minutes and in we went. "Hello Mr Levy," I said, "I'd like to introduce you to a man who composed a tune that you publish and it gets played all the time. This is Edward "Kid" Ory, and he has never gotten a dime in royalties."

"Kid! We've been looking all over for you for years. We have some money right here for you that we wanted to turn over," said Mr Levy.

They must have looked high and low for him all right. All they had to do was look in the union book. Anyhow, this Mr Levy turned over a check to Ory for around $8000 right there and then, and furthermore he got royalty checks of $600 or so every quarter from then on. That started him buying his new home.

It seemed from then on I noticed a change in Ory. At first it was nothing big, but do you know that he never thanked me for getting straight with his royalties. He never said a word. Maybe success was having something to do with it. He split from his first wife and married another woman who kind of made suggestions to him about running his band. The way they had it, after a few years you wouldn't believe it was the same guy running that band. He left his first wife in a pretty underhand fashion, but that wasn't nothing to do with me. But as far as the musicians in his band went, those guys were my friends and I didn't appreciate the way Ory treated them as time went by. I mean Minor Hall got sick when they toured Europe and they just left him without a round trip ticket and the poor guy had to get home best as he could. Wellman Braud, my old bass playing friend from Ellington's days, was on that trip and he told me they didn't get paid. Ory owed him around $200 and he had to go to the union, in other words to take Ory to the union, to get his cash. Another time I heard Ory and Ed Garland had a fist fight on the bandstand at the Hangover Club in San Francisco and Ory got knocked from the raised up bandstand on his ass. I didn't stay around till the end, but he was making a lot of enemies. He just was a different guy than I had known and helped—been glad to help in fact.

And do you know he never ever said a word about me in all of his interviews, not one good word. Not nothing at all.

I went to his funeral in 1973. They put him away New Orleans style with a band of music and some of his old buddies played for his last ride: Andrew Blakeney, Teddy Buckner, Norm Bowden, Sam Lee, Alton Purnell. I know they played *Just a Closer Walk with Thee* over him and cut out down the hill with *Muskrat Ramble* and *Ory's Creole Trombone* and that was the end of an era.

FIFTEEN

"Shoot, shoot and reshoot."

The year was 1947 and things were kind of quiet for me in Hollywood until my phone rang one afternoon. It was Joe Glaser, Louis Armstrong's manager, and he wanted to know if I would make a movie. "It'll be good. Louis and Billie Holiday will be in it and it will be about jazz," said Mr Glaser.

"Sure," I said, just figuring it would be great to work with Louis under any circumstances. "By the way, what's this picture called?"

"Oh! I almost forgot. *New Orleans*. Bye," said Glaser.

Right there, on that movie set, was where the idea for Louis Armstrong's All Stars was born. Of course no-one, not even Louis, knew at the time. He had been through a pretty mediocre period himself just prior to this movie deal coming along. He had been working as a featured soloist with big bands all over the place. He was getting tired at having to do all the playing, the show work and the general stuff involved in being a "front man."

I had seen Louis with his own big band at a place out here called the "Casa Mañana," but the band was so bad he decided to break it up. It was a terrible band he had, and Joe Glaser figured he could make more money going out by himself fronting other bands. Then this motion picture offer came up and Louis and Glaser were glad to get it. They hoped it would lead to something, and it sure did. Billie Holiday was being handled by Glaser also at the time and she was going to be in this movie too.

The film started with a guy who had written a book about New Orleans. I can't remember his name but I think his last name was Paul. Anyway they began to make a picture from his book and they wanted Louis because he was from New Orleans. Joe Glaser—he was a real hustler, that guy. He would sell anything if he got the chance, and he sold them the idea of the small band, and of Billie Holiday. So the guy that wrote the book was so disgusted at the way they spoiled the end he said he would never write for another picture. They were doing pretty good up until the end where they had that symphony band playing *St Louis Blues*. It sounded horrible.

Glaser contacted all the guys that appeared in the picture himself. The men were Louis, trumpet, myself, clarinet, Kid Ory, trombone, Charlie Beal, piano, Bud Scott, guitar, Red Callender, bass and Zutty Singleton on drums. They didn't want to hire a regular band, like Ory was running for instance, because they wanted the star names all together. Louis didn't have to suggest the men because at that time all the studio people knew about these musicians and they figured their individual names would help the picture.

Most of the guys I knew from way back, like Zutty, Ory, Bud Scott, and I had known Red Callender from the studios. He always looked so young, especially when he made that film. Of course he is quite a bass player. The piano player, Charlie Beal, I'd never heard of him before that movie, and I know about as much about him since. He had just come back to the States, maybe from the Armed Forces. He turned out to be a very good piano player and a beautiful man to work with. I knew his brother Eddie Beal quite well. He was also a piano player and worked here in the studios for years, getting the dance teams together and playing piano for them. In later years he coached Elvis Presley a whole lot through his movies.

We were on that movie around four or five weeks. You had to be there about eight o'clock in the morning and just shoot, shoot and reshoot. Louis ran the band and since we had done all the recording of the music before they actually filmed it, that wasn't no hard job. We just had to fake what we were playing as they filmed it—mime in other words. That's no big deal when you have to mime to your own playing because you know where the phrases are going to run. A couple of the songs were written out for us, like *Meet the Band*, which I think is called *Where the Blues was Born in New Orleans* on the sound track. Some composer wrote all that for us. When you are making movies you get tired of looking at the same six or seven pages of music. You start and then you have to chop it off, and then start again. Sometimes it used to take us two days to do one number. Because somebody would always come in, like the musical director, and say he didn't like a certain thing. So we'd have to change it and do it over. That was fine by us because we got paid the whole time. We made a lot of money on that set.

Things were going on pretty calm and collected until Billie Holiday arrived. For a start, she got there twelve days late. We didn't care and I know Louis didn't worry because, like I said, we got paid to just sit there until she came. I don't know why she came so late to the set, but some people, they just get a big name and figure that they come when they want. She was very big in those days, quite a star. I never worked with her before or since except for one gig in New York at the Esquire All Star awards concert. In this film they didn't fool with her at all. Mostly because she was "ornery" at the time, and kind of nasty. We made a couple of numbers behind her. I remember one was called *Farewell to Storyville* and another one was named *Endie* and that was a song I particularly liked.

Whatever else she may have been, she was not bigger than Louis. I mean they had her character all planned out in the script before she even got there, but Louis, well, they just let him be Louis. They let him have his head as to the personality he played in the film. Nobody was bigger than Louis. He was the greatest thing. Everyone knows about his greatness as an artist, but as an individual, a character, nobody could touch him. As for his talent, his mannerisms. The entire concept of the man was so natural. He could say anything and get away with it and the movie people would just laugh and enjoy it. He just played himself in all his movies.

Because the little band in the movie did so well the general public seemed to start to go for that small-band stuff again. I mean the band came over so well in the movie and the music was so great. The best number for me was one they had especially written for the film called *Do you know what it means to miss New Orleans?* It was written by two guys, Peter Derose and Ed Delage and has since became a jazz standard all over the world. In the film Louis sang it at one point and Billie Holiday also sang it.

We all got along OK on the set and Charlie Beal and Billie Holiday got to be good friends. He had the job of teaching her all the numbers from the piano, and they got along pretty good. After filming they used to go listen to records at her place. She had a little place out in West LA.

All in all I very much enjoyed the job on the film *New Orleans* and Joe Glaser seemed to have a sixth sense that that was the kind of market Louis would be having. The small-band stuff; not those big orchestras. Anyway he got the band together that same year to make some numbers that we had made in the film, for a commercial company. Zutty had left California. I think he had gone to New York—and so we got Minor Hall, out of Ory's group, to play drums. Then we made another small-band session with Louis around that same time, either a little before or a little after the one where Minor Hall took Zutty's place. This session had some of the film band's personnel and I remember Vic Dickenson played trombone. *Sugar* and *I Want a Little Girl* were two of the songs. I believe there were a couple more too.

Anyhow, Joe Glaser was beginning to think in a big way about this small-band stuff for Louis. Dixieland seemed to be coming popular with the people all over the country. Of course you could never call Louis a strictly "Dixieland" set up. He played a good number of dixieland tunes in the way the old timers used to in New Orleans. Straight lead stuff, in other words, but he also played all the tunes he had made famous in pictures. However, when the film broke up, after they completed it, I didn't have long to wait to find out that Glaser had been busy hustling.

SIXTEEN

"The All Stars."

Its a funny thing but when any person speaks about the name, "The All Stars," and there have been hundreds of such named groups throughout the history of jazz, most people immediately identify the Louis Armstrong All Stars. There is no question that the six musicians involved in that band changed the world of jazz, and I was just as proud to be part of them.

From the moment that Louis Armstrong's All Stars were formed, Louis always kept that small-band formula until he died. He had had it with big bands. He was sick and tired of doing all the work. With the small group he had more respite, and those other stars in there helped make even Louis bigger. He loved the band and said so many times. He would just stand in the wings sometimes and dig the band for himself. Like when one of the guys had their feature number; he enjoyed it like nothing else in the world and from then on he forgot all about big bands. If he had come on the scene earlier with the All Stars he might not have done any good. It was just that the time was really right. That band was to be the main group that brought jazz to the people, all over America and all over the world. The band bridged the gap between show business and art.

How the band came to be formed from my standpoint was very simple. Joe Glaser's office called and said that Joe wanted to try out something. At first it was going to be two weeks at Billy Berg's to see if the band would take off after the movie publicity. They were shooting to open around August 1947. I said that I was very interested and we agreed on a price and that seemed to be that. I loved working with Louis so anything was OK by me. They never said who else was to be in the band but only that it was to be six pieces. I didn't care who else they got, as long as it was Louis' band.

Around a week later they called again and gave me the opening date at Billy Berg's, on Vine Street near Sunset. I went to work not even knowing who else was in the band. That sounds incredible but it wasn't a deal where we had to rehearse a set programme. It was more like the old way of playing jazz. Follow the trumpet lead and feel the rest as you go along. I got there real early and Sid Catlett came in with his drums. I knew "Big Sid" just casually and then in came Dick Cary (who, incidentally, was the original pianist with the band before Earl Hines joined) followed by Arvell Shaw with a bass violin and Velma Middleton, our female vocalist. These last three had just come in from New York where Glaser had sent for them. In came Louis and Jack Teagarden. I knew Jack, as he was from out here. That was the band. Six men and a vocalist.

By the time we got to show-time the place was packed and jammed. People had been lined up all down the street. Nellie Lutcher was also on the bill those two weeks, playing half-and-half with us. She had been there before us and was a sensational performer. I'll never forget a funny thing that happened that opening night. I went out on the street for some air in Nellie's set and who should be standing out there but Gene Norman. He was the guy that later on was running the Dixieland Jubilee out here with Frank Bull. Anyways, the people were still lined up both ways around the block, trying to get in, and this Gene Norman guy says to me, "Hey Barney. Do you think it's Louis drawing all those people or Nellie?"

I looked at him, flabbergasted. "Has there been this many customers while Nelly has been here on her own?"

"Well, no!" said Norman.

"Well who in hell do you think is bringing them in then?" I asked him.

I went down and told Louis what the guy had said, figuring it would be a joke. Louis was mad as hell and after the show when Gene Norman went down to see Louis in his dressing room Louis cussed him out. So Gene was salty with me for years after that for telling Louis. I didn't care. If the guy was that stupid.

I can't remember what was the first number with the band, but it was probably *Indiana*. Louis opened the show every night for the next twenty years or more with *Indiana*. Whatever it was the crowd went for it and they came back every night for more. The business was so good that they extended the contract for another four weeks.

All this was great for Los Angeles, but Glaser couldn't figure out if he should keep the band going or not. I think he had figured, with all the business at Billy Berg's, that offers would have come in from all over.

He was still undecided when from somewhere came an offer to take the band into Chicago. We played at a place called "The Rag Doll" and people stood in lines blocks long waiting to get in. From then on we just kept rolling. It was like being back with Duke again from the traveling standpoint. I joined the band three times and left three times, in the time I was with Louis and the All Stars. It must have totaled close to ten years. The first time around was for five years anyway.

Offers were really coming in now, and the guys realized we were on to something big. We made good salaries and they kept getting better. The deal was that Louis had told Joe Glaser who he wanted, and Joe did all the hiring and firing from then on. I mean after the first band. Louis would never get involved with that side of things. The guys in that first band he kept, and he never said anything about them, any one of them, being second choice, so I guess that was his original cast. Like I said, from then on everything was left to Joe Glaser. Joe would say, "What do you think of so and so Louis?" when it came to hiring someone, and Louis would just tell him, "Oh Pops. Do what you want to do. It's all right with me."

So we were doing real good then. Not real good, damned good. Before you knew it we had an offer to go to Europe to play a festival in Nice, France. That was in 1948 and I remember then Dick Cary had to quit the band on account of family trouble. We hated to see him leave because he was a great pianist and a real nice guy. We didn't have to wait long before Glaser hired a replacement. We had Earl "Fatha" Hines join us just before the Nice Festival.

Earl had his own group, fooling around in Chicago, before he took our job, but he was glad to be part of our thing, and we were really glad to have him. In fact when Earl came in we even had a couple of rehearsals. To be truthful, it really wasn't any problem. It was just to get Louis' key or whatever. We just ran over some of our numbers. I think the reason we got such good results was because Louis just let the guys have their head. He left them on their own, especially in solos. We did all of our best stuff on the stand in front of an audience. It just wasn't one of those rehearsing bands. Like, Louis himself was a great "mugger." In other words he would always come up with something funny to say on stage. He was never caught without words, see. He played to the grandstand, but it was no put-on, just natural to him. He and Jack would be talking little things to each other during the show or he would be kidding with Velma, but always so naturally. That's what showmanship is all about. It shouldn't be forced. Louis was always spontaneous in his showmanship. It was never worked out up front.

In that way it was very different from Duke Ellington's band. With Duke we would rehearse section by section. Like one morning the reeds would get together and that afternoon maybe the brass. With Louis I don't think we had more than ten rehearsals the whole time that I was in the band. Sometimes when we had something like a movie score, or when we played a lounge show act in Las Vegas, but that was for a different reason altogether.

A lot of times we played songs that we had never played but we never could get Louis to change that *Indiana*. He knew practically every dixieland number of any era but every time we opened up he would come with *Back home again in Indiana*. Some nights he would come in and change a number in the program. You'd never know when he was going to change it either. He'd say, for instance, *Original Dixieland One Step* and we'd never played it before as a band. I was lucky because I knew most of those old standard jazz numbers but guys like Earl and Arvell, they didn't even know how the thing went. They just had to take our word that that was how it went. Louis would tell you the key and that was all. Everybody would just start going and they'd go about one round to pick up on it and by the end of the number it sounded good. Then we wouldn't play it again ever. That's just how it went on many occasions.

So anyway we went to the Nice Festival and made a pretty big hit. It seemed like just as before, when I had been to Europe with Duke many years ago, the European people were always hungry for good American jazz. Louis wowed 'em as usual but, with just six of us instead of the bigger band that Duke had, I noticed that we all seemed to be getting a greater share of attention and that made the whole band happy. When we came back from the European trip Earl had had a chance to work in to his best advantage and the band sounded real "tight" and together. This was really the "classic" period for Louis' All Stars. Just with those six men. I want to tell a little about each of them.

Jack Teagarden (trombone)

Jack was the most fabulous of men. He drank a lot—practically all the time in fact—but he always could play and never showed that liquor. You can't tell a man how to live his life, but Jack just loved that liquor. He used to take his whiskey and put it in the bottle along with one of these old benzadine inhalers, after he broke the paper off. He'd leave it for ten or twenty minutes and if he felt that liquor getting to him then he'd take this inhaler concoction and drink the whole thing down. Right quick, he would feel as fresh as a daisy. That's the way he lived, like that. He never bothered anyone. He was just a quiet man. A real wonderful guy to be around, but when he played his horn, he really played it, believe me.

I first heard of Jack when I was in New York with Duke. We had a "battle of music," as they used to call those concerts with two bands. That was the first time I saw him and, incidentally, he was too drunk to play. That is the only time I ever saw him in that shape in my life. He was actually sleeping on the bandstand and what's more it was his band. Jack Teagarden's All Star Band. So naturally I said, "Is that the great Jack Teagarden?" The guys in Duke's band that knew him had such respect for him and his trombone playing that I knew I had to be wrong. Later when I heard him play another time he really astounded me. There was no trombone player like him.

He used to be crazy about a guy called Jimmy Harrison, that played with Fletcher Henderson's Orchestra, and this Jimmy was crazy about Jack too. They used to pal around quite a bit and they stole a lot of ideas from each other. He also liked Miff Mole a whole lot as a trombone player, and, naturally, Tommy Dorsey.

See, Jack never really was right for the job of leading a band. He just didn't have the right personality for it. He was too quiet a man, too subtle. He would even speak in a Texas drawl to announce the songs. He was never in a hurry for nothing. Always relaxed to the point of seeming to be lazy. But he wasn't lazy by a long shot, it was just that when you heard him talk or play he let everything roll out so easy. He played a lot of fast stuff on his horn but I used to like to hear him play the pretty stuff. Played it just like he talked: with a drawl. Just beautiful.

He never got angry about anything, either on the stand or off it. He and Louis were friends from way back and they got along just great. Louis knew about his drinking habits, but he didn't care. It was Jack's business, you understand. Jack was a guy that never showed that liquor in his playing at all. I mean, he played the same way drunk, or half drunk, or stone-cold sober. So Louis couldn't tell him anything as it wasn't interfering with his work. I guess we all hated to see him drink so much just because we loved him so. He always had his faculties about him. I've never seen the man stumble, wallow or wave. You'd never know he was drunk. Never.

The funny thing was that Jack always drank whiskey. Straight whiskey. So he always kept a pint in his trombone case to take a nip during intermission. Anyway, Arvell Shaw found out that he had that bottle in there and he was too cheap to buy his own whiskey, so every night, just when we would be in the wings about to go on stage, Arvell would run back right quick and take a big gulp. Same thing after intermission was over too. Jack couldn't figure it out. At the end of every concert the bottle would be almost empty. He would say, "God! This bottle's almost gone. Someone must be stealing my whiskey." Of course we didn't say nothing, even though we knew who was laying into that bottle. One night Jack got smart, so before the show he half emptied the pint of whiskey and took a leak into it. He just put it back in the trombone case and carried on as usual. So Arvell took a drink from it and came out on the stand all mad. "Somebody done peed in the bottle," he yelled, right out there on the concert stage. He was mad with everyone in the band, and yet he was the one stealing the whiskey. He never stole any more, because he didn't know what in hell would be in that bottle.

Apart from his trombone, Jack's other love was steam engines and miniature trains. I remember once we were just leaving a gig in Washington, DC, and we got out by the wharf and saw this little circus. It was closing down full swing and most of the sideshows had packed up and gone, but Jack spied this little guy holding part of an engine. He watched him walk over to where he had this steam engine stashed away. So Jack went over to the man and asked him if he wanted to sell this whole big engine. The guy was glad to because the circus was going out of business. Jack gave him $200 and all he took was the thing that produced the steam and made the whistle blow. He left the rest of that junk right there.

If we played a long engagement someplace and you went into Jack's hotel room, you'd see nothing but all kinds of wires, little whistles and steam engine things. He told me that he learned about all that stuff when he was a kid. One time, we were checking into a hotel and he had this great big trunk like a sailing trunk. He had all his contraptions in there, all this iron and steel stuff. So the bus driver helped him put this trunk on the sidewalk and here came the bellboys. "Which one is yours, Mr Teagarden?" "This one, this one and this trunk." Do you know, those bellboys had to send for help to get that thing up to his room. He was quite a man.

The girls all used to flock around Jack. He had that sort of personality where they would want to "mother" him; to take care of him. They all thought they were on to something big when he would ask them to come up to see the steam engines in his hotel room after the show. Those poor chicks would just sit on the bed waiting for something to happen, while Jack laid out on the floor blowing the whistles and making the engines work.

Jack was the only white guy in the band and when we went down South he couldn't stay in the same hotel with us. We went to Norfolk, Virginia, one time and Jack used to love red beans and rice, so he had to walk all over town all by himself to find some of those beans. Apart from the separate hotels we never had any trouble in the South, and we played all over: Alabama, Arkansas, Mississippi. I heard once that in some book they say that Louis wouldn't play New Orleans on account of the racial situation there with a mixed band. Well we played New Orleans in 1949, I think, and we had no trouble. We never played any night clubs, just a concert and a couple of pre-carnival balls. In fact they crowned Louis as "King of the Zulus" which is like making him King for the Mardi Gras period. See, Gene Krupa had broken down a lot of that color shit in the South before we got there. He went to Texas to play a fair or something, and the folks gave him static about the colored guys in his band. Gene told 'em, "Well! If they don't play. I don't play." That was that. They all played.

A lot of people feel that the white boys couldn't play like the colored boys. That might have been true in the early days but it's a bunch of baloney today. It all depends on who's playing the horn. Jack was one of the greatest trombone players that I ever heard, and you take this boy Bob Havens, he is a fine trombonist. He plays with Lawrence Welk now, but he was a disciple of Jack's. In fact Jack influenced a whole generation of trombonists, just like Earl Hines did at the piano, or Louis.

Jack had a good sense of humor, but he wasn't a guy to laugh heartily. He just got his kicks out of various things. He really enjoyed the way we played *Twelfth Street Rag* with all that cornball stuff. It's on one of our records even. We were just going into it one night when he said, "Let's make a fool out of this thing." And we played it as cornily as we possibly could. Just hammed it up and it broke up the place. After that we kept it in the program just that same way.

Another thing: Jack Teagarden was a man with a great ear. And he was a terrific reader on top of that. The thing with Jack and me was we never read anything much all the time we were with Louis and he used to say to me the same thing as I told other people: "Man, this reading is just getting away from me. I must find some time to 'woodshed' it a little to get my standard back where it was." We never found time for anything in that band. We were always traveling so much. He hit ninety-nine point nine per cent of the notes that he went for. Very seldom he made a mistake or "fluffed" a note. See, he rarely tried to experiment on the bandstand or hardly ever went to making something he wasn't sure of making. He never went in for that stuff.

The only dress clothes that Jack ever wore was our band suit. He never was a guy to spend money on clothes. There was never anything flashy about the man. His best outfit was his band suit, but as long as he was presentable he didn't care. I used to love to have a chance to hear him sing too. He would sing those duets with Louis, like *Old Rocking Chair*, and he would sing things like *Please don't talk about me when I'm gone*, or *Stars fell on Alabama*. We used to stand behind him on the stage and sing, "Bricks fell on Alabama." We had so much fun with Jack in the band. His favorite song on the trombone was *Lover*. He always used to love to play that one.

Jack was married several times and had three children, I believe. One, by Addie, his last wife, was called Jack Jr and one was named Joe. I forgot the other one's name. The oldest was a handsome boy, and he was going with some oil-heiress from Texas. She was supporting him and he was playing trombone pretty good, but I haven't heard anything about him for the last few years. Maybe that money changed his mind about the trombone.

Jack had gotten an offer to form his own band and that's why he quit our band. I guess somebody talked him into believing it would be something bigger and better, but it fizzled. He kept a band going but there wasn't much made out of it. Meantime Trummy Young had replaced Jack with us. Trummy stayed for ten years or so and then he decided to go to live in Hawaii. At that time Jack was supposed to come back into our band. They had the contract all signed, and Jack was working out an engagement in New Orleans. One morning they went to get Jack from his motel room and he was dead. Just dead. That liquor killed him in the end, if you ask me. Anyway they contacted his wife Addie in Florida and she came over to New Orleans.

They flew his body out here to Los Angeles. The casket was closed because his face was so grotesque from the liquor he had been drinking. I guess they didn't want nobody to see it. The funeral was here at Forest Lawn. I was one of his pall bearers.

Earl Hines (piano)

Earl Hines was so different from our first pianist, Dick Cary. I mean, Dick is a great band piano player and plays all the right stuff, but he is strictly a musician. Absolutely no showmanship. Earl, on the other hand, sounded great with the band and was a fantastic showman in himself. He really helped sell the band from the moment he came in. When he first joined he wasn't doing too much. I think he had a club in Chicago. Anyway he started making that money again with us, plus the fact that he got more exposure from being with Louis.

He is a fine guy to get along with as long as you straighten out what you want in front. For backing, like. He never drank much but he would smoke cigars like they was going out of style. He still smokes those things almost non-stop. He used to go to sleep smoking a cigar. I recall one time we were going somewhere on a train. We shared a roomette and he stank up that whole train, never mind the roomette, with that smoke. One right behind the other. Fumes all over. I couldn't sleep all night. Of course in the All Stars there was never any smoking, or drinking, for that matter, on the bandstand. We didn't need Joe Glaser to tell us that. I mean it just looked bad and we all made that rule ourselves. If Big Sid was taking a drum solo or something then we would go off stage and smoke a quickie, or take a little nip, but as for bringing it on stage. No. Never.

Earl brought a few new songs into the band, but not too many. He had to work overtime to get used to the numbers we were already playing. He never played those old dixieland numbers for instance. When he came with us we started to play his piece *My Monday Date* every night, then he would have his solo pieces like *St Louis Blues Boogie*, or *The one I love belongs to somebody else*. That was one of his favorites. The band went up in popularity after Earl joined, of that there was no question, because he was respected all over. He had a big name himself, from a long time back.

The one thing was that they never really hit it off too well, Earl and Louis. I don't know how they got along in those early days, but with our band you could feel the animosity between them. I mean they were both band leaders to begin with. They had their ups and downs and after they would argue Earl would try to make things right with Louis. On the surface maybe he did, but Louis was like an elephant, he never forgot.

Sometimes Louis would get after Earl because he put too much show into it all and wasn't giving the soloists the support he should have. They didn't really have a good rapport together, personality-wise. It was strange to me, because they made such great music together, and had respect for one another's music. I think maybe that animosity dated back to Chicago. Both of them had been pretty popular then and maybe they were trying to out-do each other. Who knows? You understand, the main thing was that it wasn't a factor to consider too much, because they wouldn't carry it to the stand. That was something between themselves. Sometimes they got along fine, sometimes they didn't. It was one of those deals. All in all it was a great rhythm section to work with, but I think Earl felt that he was big enough to have a group of his own. Which he was.

Another thing about Earl. I don't know about now, but in those days he was scared stiff to fly. One time we were going somewhere and they had those planes with just two engines, and the engine outer covers would get red hot. Well, we took off just as it was getting dark, and Earl, he would always sit in the back seat. I think he heard that it wasn't so dangerous in the back seat. Anyway this engine started to give off a glow and Earl started to get fidgety and nervous back there. Then he saw a long red bolt of flame come out and that did it. He jumped up and ran down the plane hollering, "The plane's on fire. The plane's on fire." The steward finally got him calmed down but he put a panic in a bunch of those passengers. He was kicks.

He was a great inspirational piano player. There is still only one Earl "Fatha" Hines.

Arvell Shaw (bass)

Arvell was really just a kid when he joined us. Very young, but wild. I imagine he was in his early twenties when he joined us at Billy Berg's that first night. He was practically half the age of everyone else in the band when he joined us, but even then was a terrific bass player and a great showman. I think he was playing with Louis' big band just before it folded. I know he came from New York to join us.

He was a happy-go-lucky type of fellow. Whatever happened, it was OK with him. But one thing: he took his music real seriously. He blossomed out to be one of the best bass players around. A great asset to the band. In fact he blossomed out all around. When he joined us he was around 130 pounds and now he's about 280 pounds. He's over six feet though. Over the years he was with us he put on weight. He's as big as a house now—or should I say a mansion—but he's always a happy guy to be around. One of those fellows that is rarely "down." I don't know how much practicing he did, because we were moving around so much, but he just got better and better as the months went along. He mostly played four beats to the measure. Very seldom did he play two like those old bass players did. He didn't use too much bowed bass either, come to think about it.

He knew his way around that fingerboard though, that's for sure. He took lessons with some guy that Jimmy Blanton took lessons with, out of St Louis. That's his hometown: St Louis, Missouri. I used to kid him all the time: "Put that bass down, boy. You don't know what you're doing." He'd just laugh. He never got mad or anything, the way I'd kid him.

He always did take those long solos with the band. Right from the first night. Louis would just turn him loose because he knew what he could do on account they worked together in that big band. He'd play his ass off on *How High the Moon*. Another number he liked a lot was one that he and I did together; *C-Jam Blues*. We'd have a ball on that one. He'd take four measures and I'd take four. Back and forth. He was a real likeable young fellow and it was fun having him in the band. Arvell and our drummer Sid got along real well. They would gamble together like mad. Arvell would win all of Sid's money, every time, without fail. Finally Sid got so mad about him always winning that he threw the cards at him and they never gambled much after that little fracas. Neither one bore a grudge and they soon became buddies again later that same night. As I said, Arvell didn't worry about a thing.

Sid Catlett (drums)

"Big Sid" as we called him was the greatest drummer that I ever worked with. I had known him from Chicago, many years ago, and I was never so happy as when I walked into Billy Berg's that night in 1947 and found out that he was to be our drummer. He was so big, and he'd just sit behind those drums and you'd swear he wasn't doing anything. It all looked so easy to him. I had played with him before the opening night of Louis' band, in New York, on 52nd Street, so I knew his capabilities.

Sid was a lovable man, and I'm not saying that because he passed away. He was just lovable. He had a style all of his own. He didn't play like other drummers. When he took a solo it was like you could hear that melody line right through it all. Most guys play all those para-diddles and ratamacue stuff—all that technique stuff—but Sid tried to build around a tune. When he played *Mop Mop*, one of his features, it always sounded like "Mop Mop" because he'd have that little riff that went in there. He would knock me out. I'd be standing there looking at him and I'd shout, "C'mon Sid, let's hear it," and he would come on.

He was from somewhere in Indiana, but he lived most of his life in Chicago. He knew all the musicians and was real popular with them all. I've never heard anybody knock Sid. He and Louis got along real fine. They'd tell dirty stories on the bus to each other. Louis loved him. Even Joe Glaser got along real well with Sid. I mean we all got along with Joe, business-wise, but Sid and he were buddies. Sid could go up to that office and he and Joe would fuss about this and that. Just like "Frick and Frack," but Sid always got what he wanted.

His mind was always on the drums. He wasn't one of these guys who was always buying new things to put on his drum outfit. He just kept the same outfit all the while. The only bad thing was that many times we couldn't find him just prior to going on stage. We would be playing our theme song and out would come Sid looking all sheepish. He'd sit down at the drims and start tuning them all up, right while we were playing. Bing, bing, tap, tap. Oh! He made us all angry. He always had an excuse as to why he was late. He was a pretty good storyteller.

It was just different with Sid playing behind you. He was good for the soloist because he'd push you. He would never get in your way. Some drummers, they don't pay any attention to what's going on. But not him. He would always be "feeding" you. It's so much easier for a musician to play if he knows he doesn't have to struggle, wondering if the band is going to get faster or slower. When you get a drummer who knows all this and who doesn't interfere with you, you've got it made. Sid was exactly that kind of a drummer and one of the best time keepers. Just fantastic.

He had to leave the band because he got sick. He went back to Chicago, and next time we played there we went to see him. We thought he was getting well, but soon after he got sick again and died. I hated to see him leave the band. But those big businessmen, they wouldn't even give him a chance to get well. As soon as he'd been sick for a couple of weeks they sent out and got someone else. They could have gotten someone to take Sid's place, but no, they hired someone regular. They were so damned cold about it. Anyway they got Cozy Cole, but Cozy was so nice about it. He wouldn't take the job until he talked with Sid. Naturally Sid told him to go ahead. After a year or more I heard that Sid had died.

Velma Middleton (vocalist)

Velma was born in St Louis but her home was in New York. She used to be a chorus girl (so she told us) but when I knew her she had become a singer and entertainer. Actually, she was a mediocre singer, in my opinion, but one hell of an entertainer. Good personality and all. That's what sold her to me. She was such a great big woman, yet she would do the "splits" right there in the middle of one of her numbers. Louis would holler, "I hope she didn't break nothing." She was very well liked by audiences everywhere we went. She got so big in the end that they had to stop her from doing the splits; she was hurting herself.

She was crazy about Louis and he was the same with her. They would do those duets, like *Baby it's Cold Outside*, and break it up wherever we played. She was a wonderful person and I never heard her talk about anyone in a bad way. We'd be going out from New York on one-nighters and she would get in the bus with a whole bag full of sandwiches that her mother had fixed. They were fish sandwiches, but they tasted like no kind of fish you ever had in your life. We used to kid her, "What kind of fish is that, Velma?" And she'd say, "Buffalo." Naturally we'd laugh like mad, until we came to find out that was the proper name for 'em. Buffalo fish. Boy, I'm telling you, her mother could really fry 'em. And we'd have our jug too. We spent many a night's ride fooling with those Buffalo fish.

Velma was such a hard working girl. She had been with Louis in that big band too, right before he formed the All Stars. I guess that's how she came to know Arvell. But we all loved her. She was so big hearted.

It was a pathetic thing in Africa. We were on tour, playing one day in one of those big fields. They didn't have a bandstand but had built a big high barrack, or whatever you want to call it: big, big steps going up real high. When her time came to go on she was sick, but she never complained to anyone, so up she came huffing and puffing. Nobody really paid much attention because it was so hot anyway out there. She did her numbers and I had to go to the bathroom but I couldn't find one anywhere. I was scared to go out into the field in back of the band because of the snakes. Anyhow this English guy was backstage and he said to use his bathroom as his house was only three blocks from there. We got in his car real quick and as we were pulling out of the backstage area I heard this big commotion, like the tent covering was falling. I remember saying, "Oh boy! One of the tent poles must have broken." We went over to the guy's house and when we got back there was Velma, on the ground. There was a doctor with her who was sticking her legs. She didn't have any feeling, was glassy eyed and couldn't talk. She'd had a stroke. Right away they took her to this funny little hospital. They didn't have the facilities to treat someone like that. It was just a funny type little town, see. I felt sure that they would bring out the fire engines if necessary, to bring her to some place where they could help her.

I'll never forgive Joe Glaser and Louis for that, because they said it would take too many people to lift her on to the plane to France. I said to myself, "This woman gave her all, and they just leave her here, like that, in some little African town." She died right there in Africa.

There were many changes in the band over the period of its life but these were the main characters that helped shape the future All Stars. They were the "original cast" as they say, and I was glad to have been part of the show.

SEVENTEEN

"Like I said, there'll never be another."

As I said before, I have worked with two geniuses in my lifetime, and now I want to say a little about the other man and his music. You might think, "What more can anyone say about Louis Armstrong?" since so much has already been written and re-written, but what I can tell you is what it was like to be with the man almost night and day, on buses, planes, trains, you name it, for over ten years.

To the world, Louis was just about what he seemed. He was usually a jolly man and loved people like nothing else in the world. Or should I say, nothing but his horn and his music. He wasn't what you would call an educated guy by any means, but he had plenty of common sense and could figure out what was in your heart by just looking at you and talking with you for ten minutes. Don't forget, although Joe Glaser handled everything but the music, Louis had his share of bullshitters to listen to, too.

It has been said in print that Louis was on the surface a happy guy but really was a bad tempered, morose kind of man, and all those smiles were for show only. That is the biggest lot of crap I have ever heard. Louis was exactly the same on stage as off stage. Exactly. There never was any hidden side to him. You bought what you saw with him. He came "as is." The only thing that wasn't linked to his public image was that he sometimes would cuss people out if he thought they were trying to make a fool of him or his band. He loved his band and was happier than he had ever been with that little group. Now if somebody provoked him, that was a different thing. You'd get the greatest cussing out you ever heard, but he would have to be at the absolute end of his patience before he would ever be that way.

For instance, sometime around 1951 or 1952 we were on the road with Benny Goodman in a thing called "The Big Band All Stars," which was our two bands in a sort of road show. Benny was dying like a dog on the tour because Louis was killing him. So he tried everything to gain the prestige. He tried to get Louis to sing with his band and all. Anyway Benny called a show rehearsal when we were in NYC, or maybe it was a few days before we were supposed to open in Boston, I can't remember. He asked Louis to bring our band there to the theatre to rehearse the finale, which was *The Saints*, with the two bands. He told Louis to be there for two in the afternoon. Louis said, "Fine. We'll be there at two." When we got there, Benny had been rehearsing already so Louis says. "We're here." Benny looked at us and just said, "Yeah." That character kept us sitting around there for three hours while he carried on rehearsing his own band. I went to Louis and said, "What's with this guy? When is he going to get to our bit so we can get out of here?"

"You know, Pops," said Louis, "I'm thinking the same damned thing that you're thinking." So Louis went up on the stage and got a hold of Benny, not physically speaking though, and started calling him everything but "the child of God." He was cussing him up and down, but good. It tickled me when Louis told him, "I remember you in Chicago, when you were sitting under Jimmie Noone, trying to learn something. Now your head's got fat." So Louis just stormed out of there in a big hurry and we went right along with him. They got through the finale as best as they could.

When we got to Boston, Benny said he had heart trouble and wanted to cancel the whole tour. That could have been a beautiful tour, if Benny had been the right kind of guy. He thought he was so big that if he left the thing would collapse. All that happened was that they put Gene Krupa in front of the band, and we went on and did real good business. The tour lasted for about three months after that.

Another time we were rehearsing in New York at the same place Benny was and they had a break in their thing for about an hour. So the guys went down the street a block or so to a bar room. When they came back, Benny was standing at the door and this little bass player from Chicago, Israel Crosby comes in. "What are you doing here? You don't belong here. Get out," said Benny. "I'm the bass player in your band, that's all," says Crosby. Can you imagine that? Benny is a hell of a clarinetist, really great, but he's not the easiest guy to get along with. Gene was the opposite. An absolute sweetheart. Everybody liked him.

But Louis had so many friends. He would kid them all the time, but he was half serious sometimes when he told them things too. He was always down on Be-Bop. He was down on it till he died. He and Dizzy Gillespie were great friends. He admired Dizzy, and loved him, but he would tell him, "You don't have to play all that monkey-shine business. 'Aint nobody knows what the hell you're playing." Dizzy would just laugh at him and say, "Oh Pops, come on."

"Don't give me that Pops business. You're making all them damned notes and nobody knows what's going on. You are a musician. You know what's going on, but those people don't." Louis would say.

There's a little of Louis in all the trumpet players. I mean, for instance, he was just getting started, getting to be known for that high-note stuff. Man, they had more trumpet players around New York with busted lips, trying to make what he was making. Then they figured it must have been his mouthpiece that was doing it, so they came out with the real small-bore mouthpieces. Even that didn't help them. They just weren't in his class. In fact, when I first played with him, it was strange to be standing next to a guy that was playing way above the range of the clarinet, but after a while it didn't bother me any.

People didn't understand Louis. He just worked so hard. I've seen the time when he couldn't make a note for two weeks. One time in Chicago, at The Blue Note, he had the funny idea that there was a hair or a "corn" on his lip and he just kept picking at it. For two weeks he couldn't blow. Not one note. It was pitiful because all he would do was come out and sing. His dressing room was right next to mine and I could hear him blowing: "phew, phew." Trying, just trying. Trying. Jack and I just had to carry it, and one night a guy in the front row hollered, "Hey Louis! When are you going to blow the horn?" He was just there on stage singing, and holding the horn. He reached over and said, "Here, man. You blow it." He was really mad. With his own self more than the guy, I guess. That went on for about two weeks, then, all of a sudden, "boomp." His lip was back and he went to blowing with a vengeance.

He never believed in vacations. "Oh Pops. If I take a vacation, my lips will go down," he used to say. Once in later years when my friend Joe Darensbourg was with the band, Joe told me that they actually took a two-week vacation. Joe went home and was having a great time lying out in the sun by his pool, and the phone rang. It was the office. "You have to come back to work. Louis is getting bored just sitting around so we have fixed up some college dates right quick," they said. Can you believe that? But that's how Louis was. He was never happy sitting around. It was in his blood to blow that horn. Louis was just like Duke in that respect. Neither one could lead a normal life away from their

The recording session referred to at the beginning of Chapter Fourteen. Edward "Kid" Ory (trombone), Alton Redd (drums), Ed Garland (bass), Mutt Carey (trumpet), Buster Wilson (piano), Joe Darensbourg (clarinet), Budd Scott (guitar)

Courtesy RA

The opening night at Billy Berg's. Left to right: Velma Middleton, Barney Bigard, "Big Sid" Catlett, Louis Armstrong, Jack Teagarden (with Arvell Shaw hidden)

Courtesy FL

A publicity shot for Louis
Armstrong's All Stars

Courtesy FL

Above: Barney Bigard and Jack
Teagarden on tour with the All Stars in
Europe, 1948
Courtesy DB

Left: Members of the All Stars backstage
at a concert at Klienhan's Music Hall,
Buffalo, N.Y., 4 May 1948

The All Stars in 1952–3. Left to right: Barney Bigard, Trummy Young, unknown, Arvell Shaw, Velma Middleton, Kenny John, Louis Armstrong, Billy Kyle

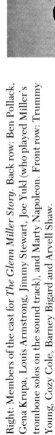

Courtesy FL

Right: Members of the cast for *The Glenn Miller Story*. Back row: Ben Pollack, Gena Krupa, Louis Armstrong, Jimmy Stewart, Joe Yukl (who played Miller's trombone solos on the sound track), and Marty Napoleon. Front row: Trummy Young, Cozy Cole, Barney Bigard and Arvell Shaw.

Left: The All Stars after Cozy Cole had joined on drums

The touring production of *A Night in New Orleans* in the mid 1970s. Left to right: Barney Bigard, Andrew Blakeney, Cozy Cole, Leo Dejan, Floyd Levin, Joe "Brother Cornbread" Thomas, Alton Purnell, Peter Müller (kneeling), Louis Nelson, Benny Carter, Sam Lee, Barry Martyn (partly hidden), Jake Porter, Red Callender, Duke Burrell, Teddy Edwards, Dolph Morris, Dick Cary, (unknown kneeling), Mario Moyal   *Courtesy FL*

music. Louis just had to be out there among people, entertaining them.

I've seen him finish a concert around eleven at night and we would all be in the bus waiting to go to the next town, and he would be in the dressing room signing autographs till two in the morning. If anyone would say, "Come on Louis," he would get cussed out right there. He would stay until he signed the last autograph. He was always good for a "touch." These musicians, old friends from New Orleans, even bums, would come to him and say, "Oh, Louis, I don't have nothing to eat with in the morning," and he would peel them off some dollars. He would tell me sometimes, "Pops, I know they are just taking me. But what can I do?" He wasn't the "spending fool" people took him for.

Louis got along just fine with everyone in the band, but he loved Jack. Of course they had their ups and downs. They would argue sometimes, but Louis never held a grudge. Of course if you did him something real nasty he would never forget it. But these little "tiffs" —he just cussed you out and forgot about it two minutes later. He never would apologize but he'd find another way. Like he'd put his arm around you and say, "Pops. Let's me and you do this or that." Louis would smoke his share of "grass" from time to time. He used to buy say $500 worth and keep it with him. Something made him quit that though. Maybe he got scared. I remember he cut that out. He would drink his brandy too. He loved brandy, and "B and B" (Benedictine and Brandy). But nothing really to excess, see.

A lot of people thought that Louis was "Uncle Tom." Well, he wasn't. That was just his natural way. He didn't care much about politics or current affairs. It wasn't that he didn't meddle in politics on account of his public image. It was just that he really didn't care. One time, in fact the only time, I ever saw him publicly make any kind of statement was on that business where they wouldn't let those little colored girls go to school in Arkansas. He cussed out Governor Faubus in public. Other than that nothing rattled him. He was the same way on stage too. I have never known him to be stage-struck or nervous. When we would come on stage he would be the last to come on. He'd just be in the wings talking or sitting there. He never got nervous. He would just come out laughing and waving his handkerchief. Sometime though he would be real sick back there, but you would never know it. He'd come out all smiles, and you thought he was having the biggest ball of his life. He probably was, but right after the show and the autographing was gone, he would go back to his ailment. Like that was the only time he could spare for it.

He could sleep his ass off too, when he wanted to. Like, we'd get on a plane and I don't care if he had slept all day before, he would sit up writing for a while and start to sleep and that would be it. He only woke up when we were going down. Long or short trips. Always the same damned thing. The longest one night hop we ever did was from Sydney, Australia, to Calgary, Canada. And that man slept the whole way. Maybe he'd get up to go to the bathroom, but then right back to sleep again. Getting his head charged.

In all the years I worked with Louis Armstrong, I never once felt that I was working with a "big star" personality. Of course, deep down, I knew that was exactly what was happening, but he was the most regular guy that you'd ever want to meet. He was nothing like, "I'm the greatest." That was the farthest from his mind. He was just one of the gang.

He was always professional—not like some of these New Orleans characters on the road today—but he never had any of those show-business affectations. He was just "a natural." You could build a show around him. You'd try to make him into something, but forget it, he was just himself. He had his own conception of how he wanted to live and that was the end of it. He never had a big head and always felt sorry for someone's bad luck. Like I said, he would dish out money at the drop of a hat. Even the ones he knew were touching him when they weren't really that bad off, even them he didn't really dislike. He would say, "Let 'em go. Poor bastards. They think they're fooling me. But it's all right. Let 'em go." That's how he was.

On the bandstand he was never interested in "hogging" the show. It just naturally seemed to belong to him. We all looked to him, and we were all happy enough. He never told you what to be playing. You just went for yourself. Sometimes he would tell you what not to play though. He never "crossed" with me. In other words, he never got off a melody note and went to a harmony note. Not ever. Once I crossed with him though. I picked on a melody note, in some tune that I didn't know, and was trying to get around. He had a keen ear and he told me to drop that particular note right quick. It was his note. Another time I was trying to harmonize on a song and he stopped me. He didn't care for the modern chord notes. He wanted the old fashioned chording. By being with Duke my ear had gotten on to some funny chord blending. Correct, mind you, but funny. He had that old New Orleans way of playing just "a melody with a beat." Sometimes he would get off lead, to play a little riff or something, but never to play harmony parts. The only time he did that was if someone was sick and we were a man short. Then he would compensate.

Louis never at any time encouraged anyone to sit in with the band. All the time I was with him I only remember one person sitting in with us. Somewhere on our travels there was a little kid that admired Louis so much. His parents brought him around and it turned out that he played trumpet and Louis was his idol. He was a nice little kid and Louis called him on the stand and introduced him to the people. He had him play a number and he was so thrilled, to be standing next to Louis. Of course he couldn't play nothing, but Louis just wanted him to feel good.

As far as Louis and Joe Glaser went, they really did get along just fine. When Louis said in an interview that Joe was the greatest man he had ever met, he probably meant it. They really were plain old-fashioned friends. Louis wasn't just saying that for business reasons.

When the good Lord made Louis Armstrong he must have "thrown away the mold" because there has never been another like him. He was truly a "man of the people." He had a hell of a sense of humor too. I remember someone asked him once, "Mr Armstrong. Do you think that jazz is folk music?" He told the guy, "Man. All music is folk music. You 'aint never heard no horse sing a song have you?" Another time he was on a plane and a guy came up to him and said, "Mr Armstrong. Do you remember me?" Louis must have been woken up by this character because he told him, "All you white folks look alike to me." When some reporter asked him to define jazz, he thought for a minute and said, "Jazz is what I play for a living." Like I said, there'll never be another.

EIGHTEEN

"From the inside looking out."

The band played its music before thousands and thousands of people all over the world but what went on behind the scenes was a great organization. This was really due to the foresight of Louis' personal manager Joe Glaser. From the inside looking out it seemed this way to me.

Joe hired and fired everybody. Whatever he did it was alright with Louis. If he fired someone Louis wouldn't say anything, even if he liked the guy real well. It wasn't on account of that he was frightened of Joe, or that Joe was a white guy handling him. It was just that Louis long ago figured that he did best out of the world if he didn't get involved with the business side. He didn't want to tread on anyone's toes or hurt anyone's feelings, so he just made no comments on anything that happened.

We had a road manager named "Frenchy" and he was the "real ass-hole" of the bunch. We called him Frenchy. I don't even think he was a real Frenchman at all. His name was supposed to be Pierre Tallerie. He had been in the Foreign Legion. I think he did some dirty work because the FBI had a running check on him. He'd tell Joe Glaser a whole lot of lies on somebody and try to get him fired. That was the one thing I held against Louis. When this guy would come to him with the papers to sign in order to fire a man Louis would just sign them and say, "Whatever Joe wants." Louis wouldn't dispute it at all. He would just keep out of it. He let that character put ideas in Joe Glaser's head about people. He was always running to Joe with some tales. There wasn't anyone in the band that liked him. Louis tolerated him, I suppose. I always used to ask him, "What do you keep that man for? He 'aint doing nobody any good, at least not in the band. Or anyone else for that matter." "Oh Pops. Don't pay him no mind. He's just an old bus driver," Louis would say. He might have been only a bus driver but he was saying all kinds of things about Louis behind his back too. Even the manager of one of the places we played told Louis, "What kind of man do you have for your road manager? He is out there low-rating the band and telling all kinds of lies." I really wanted to beat the hell out of him a couple of times.

One time much later, when Cozy Cole was playing drums with us, Cozy and I were in a restaurant. It was around Christmas and we were either in Los Angeles or getting near to it. We were sitting eating and over comes this Frenchy, so I said to him. "You see. We're going into LA. A great big town like that and you don't know what to do. You don't have any friends." "I don't need any friends. My friends is my money," he says. So when we got to town I had an apartment over on 8th Street and I invited Cozy over for Christmas. Dotty had fixed a big dinner. The phone rings and it's this Frenchy. We were having a ball, just getting ready to eat, and this son-of-a-bitch starts hinting around. He was trying to muscle in and be invited around. I told him, "Go eat with your money," and hung up on him. Cozy said, "Yeah. That's nice. He don't need no friends." He was with the band for years until he finally died of a brain tumor.

At first Joe Glaser himself used to go out with the band, like as road manager, utility man and whatever else was necessary. He kept building up the band and then the travel got to be too much so he stayed in the office in New York and sent other people out with us. He was slick, because when they would call for Louis to appear somewhere he would tell them that Louis was all booked up, but they could have him later in that year if they took so and so now. That kept his whole stable in work. He was a hell of a business man. I don't think anyone else could have taken Louis as far as he did. I got along just fine with Glaser, but he thought I was kind of wild, crazy, so he left me alone. It was account of one time we went overseas, and I had been traveling so much, I was dead beat, and wanted to stay home. He told me that if I went he would give me a bonus when I got back. "Don't tell the other guys. Just drop in any time you get back and I'll see you have your bonus." Those were his words. So I made the tour and when we got back to New York, I went up to the office to get my "bread." He had seemingly forgotten all about it and he started cussing and throwing a fit in the room there. When he really swore at me I told him, "Listen I don't have to take this from you. Goddammit, I'll throw you out of the window." I got my bonus OK but he thought I was crazy for threatening to throw him out of the window and we got along just fine after that. I took him as a man of his word. I only wanted what he had promised me.

Joe never discussed music with me or anyone else in the band. In fact I never ever talked to him about anything that happened in the band. That was none of my business. Strictly between him and Louis. See, Joe would have the ideas, not Louis, and naturally he had to clear it with Louis first. It was Glaser's idea, for instance, to record the album we made, *Satch Plays W. C. Handy*. That was strictly Joe's idea. I guess he had sold some company on the idea, and in fact the record did real well for everyone concerned. We were somewhere on tour and I recall we took the tapes round and played to the old man. W. C. Handy, I mean. He just started crying. He cried all through the tapes. It meant a whole lot to him.

So that was how Joe Glaser and Louis got along. Just like that. They seemed to make it on through with that arrangement. It wouldn't have suited me. I wouldn't have no manager telling me what to do and what not to do. I'd have gotten rid of any such guys a long time ago. Louis didn't stand up for the men against Joe, except for one time. It was much later. Mort Herbert was playing bass with us and Joe was firing him. I know Arvell Shaw was supposed to come back with us and take Mort's place. So they brought the papers for Louis to sign and he told them, "You're going over my head. That boy is not going to leave here at all. He's going to stay right here in this band." They kept Mort after that. That's the only time I saw Louis go against Joe's wishes. I don't know why. I mean Mort was a terrific bass player and so was Arvell, but something just must have gotten to Louis that particular night. But like I said. They got along just fine that way. Joe ran the business; Louis ran the music.

The band always lined up on stage the way Louis wanted it. He was in the center and Jack and I were either side. The drums would be in the back in the center and the piano right behind Jack, the bass right behind me. I had always felt I should have been in the center by the main mike because that brass was so powerful. Sometimes they would overpower me and I would crowd that mike like the devil. I don't know why he had poor little me right out on the end, but that's how he wanted it. In the same way, I'll never know why he had the bass so far from the piano. He once told me that it was because he wanted good rhythm. Once they started, he wanted them to keep the same tempo. The drum was the main tempo setter for Louis and he didn't want the piano and bass to gang up and crowd the drum. See that's where he got his stuff into the number, just by paying attention to that drum beat. With Sid Catlett they couldn't go nowhere, but if they did they would catch hell from Louis. He was very strict on tempos. Generally the piano would give four bars or eight bars introduction and the drum would pick up in those bars, then the whole band came down together.

We had no special soloing order on every tune like some bands do. I mean the solos came in different places in the first number we played, than the second or third numbers. See? Louis would just lean over and say, "Take it Jack," or "Blow some, Barney." But once we did establish a set routine of solos on any one particular number, then it stayed the same way.

A lot of times I felt the band to be unbalanced. I mean those endings where Louis would really be up high there blowing like mad. Jack would be bearing down too, and many times I had to rush to that mike just to be heard in those "out choruses." All in all I would describe the All Stars as a polished band. You could take a lot of men using the same instrumentation as ours and they wouldn't be so polished. Everyone in our band had their own conception of what they wanted to do, but it had better come out good as a whole or Louis would get after you.

A lot of times Louis would bring in things that I had never heard before. I would lay dead and just fish around trying to find a part. He had the melody line down, so that was no big problem for me. I'd just listen to what was going on until I got the tune and the chords in my head. I knew most of those old New Orleans tunes anyway, but sometimes he would come in with a pop song that he had recorded, like *Blueberry Hill* or one of those. That wasn't the problem. It was when he just hit on a song that he had heard and liked that had me scuffling. We never had any music in that band and only a bi-annual rehearsal at best. I was sorry, in a way, because that was what ended my days of reading music. Never again after Louis could I read from sight. I just let it slip away.

NINETEEN

"Guys came and went, but the band kept on going."

The first guy of the "original cast" to go was Sid Catlett. Cozy Cole came into the band. He got to be a real good friend and we had lots of laughs together. We are still real good friends, thirty years later. He was as good a drummer as Sid in a lot of ways, even better in some, but his timing was not so much to my liking as Sid's was. Of course it was hard for him to come into a band already formed and tight, for a start. He did a real good job and was an excellent showman. He was and is the most amiable guy. He was always practicing, all on the bus, in the hotel room, everywhere we went, out would come that practice pad. Once he was practicing in the hotel for so long, late at night, that a couple of us couldn't sleep so we called the desk and complained to the manager, for a joke. The manager went up to his room and gave him a bad time. When we got in the bus next morning Cozy says, "You know what? Some lousy bums called the manager and complained about the noise I was making last night."

"Well I'll be damned," I said, "Sneaky bastards. Whoever would do that to a musician." We had some fun with him, I can tell you.

Cozy wasn't too sure of those New Orleans cadences we used in the band to bring in a funeral march, or a six-eight, then pick up to the main part of the song. Louis and I both knew what to do because we had played funerals and such before we left home, when we were young. We had this one number, where we opened with a funeral dirge *Flee as the bird to the mountain*, and we would all march across the stage then Louis would hit "Ta ta, Ta ta" on the horn and the drums picked up time, just like those old timers did in New Orleans. We schooled Cozy on how it went and once he had it down, he sounded as if he'd been doing it all his life.

About a year or two after Cozy joined we made a movie with the band called *The Strip*, starring Mickey Rooney. I don't know why, but Cozy wasn't in that film with us. There was a guy out here called Smokey

Stover that played with us in *The Strip*. The rest of the band was the regular bunch: Louis, Jack, myself, Earl, and I'm not too sure if Arvell played bass or not. Anyhow, the story-line was built around Mickey Rooney wanting to play in the band with us at a night club owned by the actor William Demarest. The first couple of reels had Smokey Stover actually playing drums, and then the story line went to show that he left us, and in came Mickey Rooney. That little guy was really talented. It was actually him playing drums on the set right with us. He was something else. He loved the band. He'd tell the director, "Come on. These boys are tired, let them rest. Let's take the afternoon off." Then he'd go and get some little chick and take her out and screw her. All those movie people had their own private little places around town, but Mickey always had a chick at his.

Nobody made arrangements for the music we played in that movie. I remember there was one number called *Shadrack* that we had to play. We just had "skeleton" parts. We only had to find out where the breaks came and Louis would smile into the camera and say, "This is Barney Bigard" or "This is Jack Teagarden." He'd just introduce us like that. That movie often comes on the "late shows", even now, but to tell the truth, I was never much interested in the movies I made so I never watch them.

The next guy to leave was Earl Hines. See, guys came and went, but the band kept on going. Marty Napoleon played piano with us for a while and then Billy Kyle came into the band. In my opinion, Billy Kyle was the best piano player Louis ever had. He was strictly a band man. Just straight comp. Of course he could solo too. Sometimes we would turn him loose on a number by himself. One that he used to feature himself on a lot was *Pretty Little Missy*, which he wrote. I think he was perfectly suited to the All Stars.

The last guy that came into the band before I left was Trummy Young. You see, I left the band three times. Once for a year or so, the next time for four years and then I finally left in 1961.

Anyhow, Trummy Young joined after Jack Teagarden. They had a guy called Russ Phillips in there for a short while, but he didn't work out so Glaser got Trummy. He had a hard job filling Jack's shoes, but he made it, and even added to the trombone parts in the band. I really enjoyed working with him. Of course he was more powerful than Jack was—more "brassy"—but that meant I had to fight that team even harder on the clarinet. Louis and Trummy were a hell of a brass team. Trummy was real quick to catch on. He was, and is, a fantastic trombonist. He'd drive you, and make you feel good. Of course Jack could swing too, but Trummy was more "brash" when he would pump something out, then he could turn around and play the sweetest stuff right behind. Maybe it was all that working with Jimmie Lunceford that gave him that great tone. I had a lot of confidence in Trummy. We all knew what he could do, and he sang too, which helped the band go over. He just filled in perfectly all the way round.

Sometime around the middle of 1952, I think it was, I started getting sick of the traveling and of always being on the move, so I gave my notice in to that "fat-bellied" Frenchy and went home to take a long rest. I really did rest most of the time. It was good to be off the road for a while. The time I was out of the band they got a guy from Texas called Bob McCracken to play in my place. I didn't really know if I would be happy doing nothing or not. I guess the ideal thing would be to play five or so years in a band that you loved to work with, and take the sixth year as an overdue leave of absence, then see if you wanted to go back to the band. In jazz, the ideal very rarely happens, but you can always count on the unexpected.

I had been resting for a period of six or seven months, working the Hollywood studio scene, when the phone rang one day and it was Glaser's office. They wanted to know if I would consider coming back with Louis. I guess by then I had had my share of sitting around, so I told them yes. I believe it was in mid-1953 I rejoined Louis and the All Stars.

When I came back to the band that second time around things were pretty much the same as when I had left. We still opened up with *Back home again in Indiana*. Nothing had changed. In a way I was glad to be back with the old gang. One thing was that I noticed we had made a whole lot of new fans. Louis was really very, very big through the last twenty years of his life. He had made a lot of friends, fans and admirers in the Hollywood Movie crowd. Maybe since we got around when we were making that movie *The Strip*. Anyhow, a lot of people would come to hear the band when we played in Los Angeles and one of these guys was Dick Powell, the actor. Dick was a real swell guy, and so was his wife, June Allyson. They were thrilled to come and hear the band play, and they came many times too.

Later in that year of 1953, June Allyson made a picture with us. It was called *The Glenn Miller Story*. In fact I have a picture on my wall now that she signed for me. She was a real sweetheart. The movie was real fun to make. James Stewart played Glenn Miller and June played his wife. Jimmy Stewart didn't really play the trombone on the sound track, that was done by a guy named Joe Yukl. After the movie came out he actually went on a tour on the strength of playing in the picture for Jimmy Stewart. All we really did with the band was to record the music for a night club scene and then we had to act a little for the cameras when they synchronized it. I think Stewart and Gene Krupa came down to this cellar sort of place and we jammed a little together. I know that Cozy and Gene had a drum battle going for some time. In fact, a little after we made the film Cozy left the band and went into a drum school business with Gene. I was real sorry to see him go.

We got a guy in there to replace Cozy. His name was Kenny John. He was a real young guy who drank plenty, but could play good drums. We made a recording with him that was supposed to be a follow-up to *The Glenn Miller Story*. I know they had *Basin Street Blues* as one of the titles and Kenny had to kind of emulate the drum battle sequence from the movie all by himself. He was a nice little guy. He tickled me. He would come on stage ten minutes before curtain up and throw a glass of water on his bass drum head. He didn't want a drum sound; he wanted a straight "thud." We got another drummer after Kenny John quit the band. I liked him very well, what he was doing, that is, but he was a little crazy. Crazy in a nice way. He was really a real nervous guy. His name was Barrett Deems. He stayed with the band for a good while, and he's still a hell of a drummer.

During this time a lot a "big shots" would come to listen to the band. One guy that was a fan was Fred Astaire. I had made a movie with him back in the forties and he would sometimes come out to hear us. Every time I'd see him (he had a turkey farm near San Diego, by the way) he'd say, "When are you going to come out and get a turkey. It's on the house." I never did find time to go out there, but if I had I know he would have kept his word. He was a great guy to be around.

You see, when we made movies you never knew what Louis would do. He would do practically anything and get away with it. He was recording a thing with Bing Crosby one time for a movie. They were going to do *Sleepy Time Down South*, and it had the word "darkies" in the lyric. The man in charge didn't want that in there so they changed the word from "darkies" to "folks" and did the whole thing over. Louis was so "teed off" at having to keep re-recording, that finally when the end of the day came, and it still wasn't "in the can," he told them he wouldn't come back the next day. Of course he did come, but he walked straight up to Bing and said, "What do you want me to call those black sons-of-bitches this morning?" Like I said, he said anything that entered his head.

It seemed like twenty years that I played with Louis the second time around because of the touring schedules. Actually it was only two years, but things had gotten harder because Louis was always getting more and more popular. That meant we had to work twice as hard to satisfy the people. It was getting to be a drag again, on the road for months on end, and so I decided that I would quit once and for all. I gave in my notice when we were somewhere near Los Angeles and went home again.

Joe Glaser got Edmond Hall in my place and Louis seemed satisfied, so I didn't have any feelings of "letting the guys down." Edmond was a real fine clarinet man, and in fact was a more forceful player than I was. We were buddies because I had met him years ago in New York, but without doubt he was the "cheapest" man I knew. He used to live in a place where he had to walk up so many flights of stairs to get up there, just to save rent. When Edmond got into the band they were going on a tour to France so I asked him to pick me up a couple of boxes of reeds that they make over there. He said that he would, and so when the band came back they played out here in California and I went to see them. Edmond said, "Man. I got your reeds." You know that he wouldn't turn loose that little box of twenty-five reeds until I had given him the money. He was like the duck's ass. Water tight.

Anyway, I gave the chair over when we finished at Gene Norman's place in Los Angeles, and went back to resting good, eating good, all the little things in life that seem impossible when you are out on the road. I didn't know what I was going to do from then on, and frankly, I really didn't care. I just wanted to spend two nights in the same bed for a change.

TWENTY

"Play your own way."

Dottie's mother had a place down in Vista, California where she raised avocado pears. She had a whole grove of trees and we decided to just go live down there for a while and the hell with the music business. We stayed down in Vista about six months just crawfishing and picking avocados. Vista is a place down near Oceanside and it is supposed to have the most even climate of any place in the world. Lots of athletes retire down there and go to farming avocados. I had plenty of time to think things over, about my music and my life so far. We didn't even go into town to hear music through this period. I just wanted to get away from it all and see if I could be happy. I had plenty of time to philosophize.

I don't really have a philosophy, then or now, for that matter. Just some thoughts. I asked myself if I still had the drive and ambition that I used to have. After thinking about it I figured that I could still execute on my clarinet, and I still had lots of ideas on music running through my head. I would get out the horn once in a while to run over a few licks but not like I used to twenty years before. Then I would practice three to four hours every day. I guess a lot of my early incentive had gone.

One time I even sat down to read some of my old press write-ups that Dottie had kept. It's funny. All the years on the road I never read them and here I was looking through them with interest. I used to buy *Downbeat* magazine all the time but once I read that Pee Wee Russell had won a *Downbeat* poll. That did it. I never read that magazine again. Guys like him and that Frank Teschemacher aren't clarinet players to me. But then I suppose even in those days critics were just as ignorant as they are today. I never, ever, played to please the critics. Not once. I never really cared about them at all. Even today I still don't. I mean you can pick up a music paper and read them knocking all of the old-style New Orleans musicians that are currently out doing their thing. To me it was just beautiful to see those old guys, at their age,

126 / WITH LOUIS AND THE DUKE

coming out on stage and doing a lot of things the youngsters can't do. Most people forget that those guys are the foundations of jazz music. They started it, but naturally everything progresses as it goes along. It's like the Wright brothers' plane. Now you could throw a rock and knock it out of the sky, but for Christ's sake give them credit for building the first. Musicians nowadays have gotten a lot better learning than the old musicians could have had. The kids have every advantage to becoming a good musician, and after they get their learning they try to play on the order of the older men that went before. You see a lot of that. It's not wrong.

The only thing I say is to play like your own self. Don't be copying someone else. Try to create a style of your own and then stick to it. Any of the big names have their own style. You can always tell a Louis Armstrong or a Teagarden or a Hodges, but when you get down amongst the lesser ones it's hard to tell them apart. I tell all the young guys I meet, "It's good to take influence from someone, but don't play note for note like them. You'll never make it in this racket. Play your own way."

Another thought that occurred to me. You read all kinds of stuff about the jazz in Europe being so great. I think the only great jazz musician to come out of Europe was Django Reinhardt, the guitarist. He was the only completely original one that played jazz in the American way, with that same swing. Most all of the other musicians seem to take practically all their stuff from records. It's that lack of originality that worries me. They don't have the same feeling as Americans have. Maybe in time they will get it. Only time will tell. But this Reinhardt guy was unbelievable. I recorded with him in Europe on one of my trips and, as I said, he was a complete original. Even today his talent has never been matched but in those days he stood out alone.

People have asked me over the years who would I choose if I could pick a band of my own from all of the great musicians I ever worked with. Looking back, the answer is easy. I would have to take Louis Armstrong on trumpet, Jack Teagarden, trombone. The piano would be simple; I'd take Billy Kyle. I loved his solo work, but as a real "band" pianist he was unequalled. On bass, Jimmy Blanton for sure, and drums, no question, Sid Catlett. That would be my choice. Another thing is that all these men had their own style; they knew their horns and they were easy to work with. That's a thing that holds so many musicians back. I never figured myself as being a "temperamental" musician. I put myself down as easy going and I think that helped my career a lot. I was never one to care who had top billing, or who played the last act. Some guys, that was all they thought about. I just wanted to be good at what I did. I wanted to get jobs that were in my category. I didn't want to be no symphony man. If I had devoted all my time to that then I wouldn't have been a jazz clarinetist. I did want to be a *good* clarinetist though. Just to read enough music to get me by. That's the way I always felt. I never thought of myself as an artist, or anything like that. Just as a good jazz player that always tried to do his best. Of course I try to live up to my own standard of playing. Sometimes it materializes, sometimes it doesn't, but I keep trying anyway. I would hate to say I was all set on the horn. There is always something more to learn. And you can't stay away from music for long—at least I couldn't.

So, like I said, sitting around those months in Vista looking at avocados I had all the time in the world to think about what I was going to do and finally I decided that I just couldn't sit around not blowing my horn much longer. As it was, a voice from the past kind of took me by surprise and I might say fate took a hand. Kid Ory's first wife Dort called us and said she was going to have surgery. She had been a good friend for many years and I think she just wanted someone to kind of "hold her hand" through the troubles. We came back to Los Angeles to look after her.

TWENTY-ONE

"I was never destined to rest for long."

I liked being home. It was a good feeling. We had an apartment in the Wilshire District and Dotty and I found the adjustment from all that traveling and from the "small town" environment real refreshing. It seems like I was never destined to rest for long, because a guy named Ben Pollack called me to come to work at his place on Sunset Strip.

Ben was a drummer who had had his own band for years. He had so many talented guys come through his band ranks. Guys like Benny Goodman, Glenn Miller and people of that stature. Of course they were the big stars in these years, that is the years I'm talking about now, but Ben wasn't doing too much himself. Years ago he had a great band with Nappy Lamare, Yank Lawson and those fellows, but for some reason, they all quit Ben and took Bob Crosby on as a front man and formed the "Bob Crosby Bob Cats." They did real well with that group but Ben continued on without so much recognition. During the forties he had worked as a booking agent for bands and even as a director for an act that Chico Marx had. He also owned a fairly successful record company for several years, by the name of "Jewel Records." With all this going on, I guess he put away some of his bread and that's how he came to open a night club in the fifties.

So Ben had this place up on the "Strip" and it was called Ben Pollack's Pick-A-Rib. He was doing terrific business. He would stay open until two in the morning and just lay for all those Hollywood big shots that would come in. See, they could drink, hear jazz and he had a chef that could fix ribs like nobody's business. It really was a good thing that he had going there. All the movie stars would come there to eat. That kind of a place. It was right on a corner and the parking lot was way down the hill. It was a drag for us walking all up that hill every night but we had some fun in there.

I was freelancing after I left Louis, and Ben called and asked me about working at his club. I was glad to do it. We all had separate prices in that band. In fact, to tell the truth, it really wasn't a band. It was called "The Pick-A-Rib Boys," and Ben would call different guys every night. The best thing for me was that he had Jack Teagarden and me as regulars together. We didn't work every night, but sometimes four or five nights each week. It was great to be back with Jack again. I loved to play with him. Sometimes Ben would play drums with us but mostly he would hire a guy to play and then maybe he'd play for the last set himself. I was glad he didn't play all the time because he had such a heavy foot on the bass drum. My, he was loud on that bass drum stuff. Maybe it was because he had laid off for so many years, who knows? He used to love to hear me play in the low register. He'd holler from back of those drums, "Play that low one for me Barney," and that heavy foot of his going all the time. He was a right kind of guy though. I liked him and he did a lot for musicians out here. Billy Berg wasn't operating any more see. They had him on the unfair list for some damned silly reason and he had gone down a lot. He tried to get back but he couldn't make it. That's when Ben came on the scene and a lot of the old crowd that hung around Billy Berg's were coming in to us at the Pick-A-Rib.

Ben had a couple of crazy notions about running the place. I never tell a guy what to do, but I hate to see a guy doing something that he could do much better. He never did advertise the band at all, outside or in the press. He had Jack Teagarden and me from Louis Armstrong's All Stars, and that alone could have brought him in some additional trade. He didn't seem to care. The other damned stupid thing was that he never applied for a singing license, and so the great vocals of Jack Teagarden were never heard in Ben Pollack's.

Soon Jack and I were working there every night. I guess Ben liked us. They changed the piano players around all the time. Marvin Ash was there a lot, I know that. George Orendorf played trumpet there a load of times with us. Of course if you look at it one way, Jack and I had Louis in the middle of the two of us for years, so any trumpet player would come off with a hard job. George Orendorf could play good then and he did a great job. We also had Manny Klein a lot, playing trumpet. They were the two main ones I remember.

Any time we got a better gig, any of us, we would tell Ben and he'd give us the night off. It was pretty good working in there for him, but then Jack left and I got tired of carrying things on the stand. Jack had decided to put his own band together again and he wanted to start touring again. He asked me to join him, but I was happy in Los Angeles and so I declined his offer. He kept that band operating until he died in New Orleans in 1964.

Maybe it seemed like a good idea but the thought occurred to me that if Jack could front his own band and tour all over the country, maybe I could do the same but keep my group nearer home; just tour through California and the bordering states. Since all of my connections with the Joe Glaser office, or Associated Booking Corporation as it is known, were still fresh I decided to form a group and have them handle the business, if Joe agreed. That he did, and my bookings were handled by Bob Phillips, the West Coast executive of ABC.

Now I had the management end set, I had to get me a band. I hired five other guys and we were all set. Burt Johnson was my trombonist. He had been with Charlie Barnet for a good while. I liked him. He played a lot like "Tricky Sam" from my Ellington days. All that plunger mute stuff. Then I got a guy called Jackie Coons on trumpet. He was good too, really good. The only reason Jackie never had a break with the big-name bands was because he drank too much. When he worked for me I told him flat out, "Don't be drinking on my stand. You act right. Do your drinking afterwards." I never had any trouble with him. I got me a real good piano player named Bruce McDonald. I had met him before in the years with Freddie Slack. In fact, we were already good friends when he joined the band. My bass player was Bobby Stone. I had known him since the war and felt really happy with him. In fact when I first worked with Bobby in the war years he wasn't eighteen yet. I had to pass him off as eighteen though, so he could even get in the place to work. The last guy I got was Charlie Lodice the drummer. He had a good beat and was plenty lively. In fact later in years he moved to New Orleans and became a member of Pete Fountain's band. These guys with me were practically all youngsters but good musicians. I really just wanted to have a little fun for myself and it worked out real good. I had a good band.

So the year of 1956 saw me leading my own band. We played some nice little music. Good arrangements of various pop numbers like *Little Coquette* or *Blue Skies*. Stuff like that. A guy called Johnny White did some of these arrangements for us.

One thing we did with this band, apart from making three nice residences in Las Vegas, incidentally, was that we made a real nice record for Liberty Records. One of the numbers I remember on that album was a song I put together called *Louisiana and Me* which I liked a lot. That was the craziest deal, that Liberty record. Howard Rumsey, the bass player who owns the "Lighthouse" down in Redondo, was the one who contacted me about making that album. I guess he was their A and R man at the time. He took me to see the guy that owned Liberty Records and this guy set up a deal with me. I guess we should have entered up a contract there and then, but they wanted to get the record made so fast that I took the guy at his word and we made the recording date. Everyone was jubilant about the session; about how good the band sounded and the good spirit the session had. So I went to the guy to get the rest of my money. He had given me part of it up front, but he still owed me over half of the bread. He told me that he had promised no such thing about any more money. Howard Rumsey was there when the deal was made and he didn't have nothing to say about the shabby way they were treating me. I told this character that I would sue him and had my lawyer Charlie Weintraub start to draw up the papers.

He said that, as owner of the company, he would give me 5% of the records sold and not the cash price we originally agreed on. "That's how Crosby and Sinatra work," he said. "I can't afford to work that way," I told him. "They sell millions of albums and so 5% of all that adds up. I just want my goddamn money to pay off my men." Anyway with all this hassle going on he decided to let up on the whole thing. It never got any distribution and therefore never became anything to speak of commercially. It's a real shame because it was such a good session and it was well recorded—at Capitol Studios in fact. On top of that it was the first long-play album I ever made under my own name, for all the good it did me though.

While I was on a job in Palm Springs a strange thing happened. A jazz musician had a number that went straight to the top of the American Hit Parade. I'm talking about my old buddy Cozy Cole and his number *Topsy*. Very few times in the history of jazz has one of our own had a number one hit. Of course Louis did from time to time, especially in later years, but this was around 1959. Cozy had recorded this number, which was just a riff and then an extended drum solo that went the length of the record until the riff came back and closed it out. It just took off and so, quite naturally, Cozy had to put together a band and do a follow-up tour.

He called me to join his band for the "after the hit touring" and I told him I would take the trip or trips with him. We had been good friends since we worked together in Louis Armstrong's All Stars and so I knew we would have some kicks playing together again. Actually the band wasn't so hot. He had Lennie Johnson, I remember, and some half-assed organ player and a lot of guys that I just cannot recall. Joe Glaser wasn't doing the bookings. It was some other outfit.

So I left Dottie managing the apartment house and went out on the road again. We played all kinds of engagements with Cozy Cole's Band: concerts, dances, anything. It was easy to book the band because *Topsy* was playing on all the juke boxes from Coast to Coast. I got so tired of playing it though. Sometimes we would play it once in each show, and we generally played three shows each night. We played at one great big outdoor concert in Philadelphia and thousands and thousands of people showed up. Fred Waring and his Pennsylvanians were on it too. We did plenty of traveling with that band, I do remember that part of it all.

Over the Christmas holidays of 1959 we were in Chicago working at some night club and Dottie came out to join me. Louis Armstrong was at "The Palmer House" and they finished earlier than we did so Trummy Young and Louis and Marty Napoleon came over to catch our last set. After the thing was all over we sat and talked for a couple of hours. I realized how much I missed being around Louis and Trummy and that kind of music just by listening to them talk. Trummy told me that the clarinet player that was with them at the time, Peanuts Hucko, was thinking of quitting and that I should be prepared for a call from the office. Sure enough within a couple of weeks I got my call and told them I would come back with Louis Armstrong and the All Stars. This was the third time I had joined the band in a lifetime and because it had been so long I was a little apprehensive about what they would play. I didn't have to worry long about that though as I would be on the bandstand soon enough.

TWENTY-TWO

"Five years later it was still *Indiana*."

When I played my first job with Louis after being out of the band for so long I asked him, "What are you going to open up with Pops?" "*Back home again in Indiana*," he said. Five years later it was still *Indiana*. Nothing had changed too much; the front line was just as good but the rhythm section wasn't as good by a long stroke. I didn't like the rhythm section so much on account of the new drummer Danny Barcelona. Billy Kyle was his old spirited self and Mort Herbert, the new bass player, was all right but Danny was the one. He was flashy, he could excite the people because he was so small and they thought he was a little boy. He was about forty years old at the time I came back but those kind of people just don't mature; they don't get old looking. I couldn't see anything special about his playing but I just didn't pay much attention. He was a real nice guy though. Trummy and Louis were as good as ever and it felt like old times to be back playing with them again.

One thing I enjoyed during this last period that I played with Louis was a special recording that someone had organized for Duke Ellington to play with Louis' band. It was fun for me to be recording with the two most important bandleaders in my career at one session. To tell the truth, I think Billy Kyle fitted in Louis' sound better than Duke did, but for that date it all turned out OK. Duke and I reminisced a while before we started, but the main thing was that Louis got along so great with Duke. I mean two prominent leaders on one date could have been rough, but we had no problems.

Duke was playing a lot of his own numbers and not the things that we generally used to play with the band at that time. It was his session and I guess it would be fair to say that he really took over. It wasn't so much that he did the talking but, as I said, they were mostly his tunes. The session came out real well.

During all the traveling I always took Dottie along in this period. She was the only wife that traveled with the band. We didn't have any children and she figured her place was with me so I was glad to have her along. In fact one of the best things came along in this period in 1960. We were going to make a tour of Africa, but before that they wanted Louis to make a picture in France called *Paris Blues*. They didn't want the whole band, just Louis. They figured that since we would be coming through Paris on route to Africa they would hook it all up together. I guess the film must have ran overtime because the whole band went to Paris, and because they were only using Louis we got a six-week vacation in Paris, with full pay. Dottie was really pleased because she met up with an old friend named Flo, and they saw all the sights courtesy of the Joe Glaser empire. Flo was the secretary of the Los Angeles Dodgers Baseball Team. They had a ball, and I got to see some of my French friends like Claude Luter and Maxim Saury. It was a good time that Parisian vacation.

Louis had his own private doctor who traveled with him most of the time although he didn't go out of the States too much. His name was Doctor Alexander Schiff. Doc Schiff was a little slight man who was a friend of Joe Glaser. He had been a doctor for the Boxing Commission at one time and lived in the same apartment building as Glaser. He loved Louis and would take real good care of him. If there was anything wrong that he couldn't handle, then he would recommend Louis to a specialist somewhere. It was good to have him along with us.

We finally made it to Africa and played over there the remainder of 1960. We played places such as Kano, Doula, Kinshasa, Entebbe and all kind of places that I can't remember. It was a strange trip because the Mau Mau were quite active all the time we were there. We really didn't get too bothered by any bad things happening but it was strange to be in a country at the time of so much going on internally with the politics and all. We did most of the internal travel by small planes and it was plenty hot. Africa wasn't my idea of the greatest place on earth but it was OK once you got used to it. Trummy, Billy and Louis had been there before on a trip when Edmond Hall was with the band and so they could get around a little, but I got used to it.

One day I just sat up in my motel room and reflected on the life I was living. Always on the road, living out of a suitcase, dragging my wife around all over the world. It dawned on me that I was fifty-five years old and I had been careful enough with my money to put a little by for that "rainy day." I thought a great deal about leaving the band for the third time and finally came up with the answer that I had done enough traveling to see half the world, and could really retire to playing when I felt like it and not seven nights a week if I didn't. That was getting to be a drag the older I got. Sometimes you just don't feel like going out on that stage and blowing. Louis, now, he was a different man. Nothing in this world would he rather do than be out there, day in, day out, blowing and entertaining. On the other hand, I wanted to do a little composing, which I never found time to do with the band schedule. I wanted to go home and laze around catching crawfish and catching up on all manner of things. My brother Alex was still down in New Orleans trying to make a living selling insurance and playing drums on the side, but he wasn't doing so good and I had to try and help him as best as I could. I knew that if I quit Louis again it would be the last time because even the guys in the band would get tired of me, in and out.

Having weighed the whole thing up, I gave in my notice for the last time in July 1961 and finally, for good, left Louis Armstrong and the All Stars.

I recommended a good friend of mine and a fine clarinetist named Joe Darensbourg. He had been with Kid Ory during most of his comeback and was familiar with all the songs Louis played. He was working at Disneyland at the time and he flew up to some little town or other to join them. I was supposed to catch a plane home an hour after Joe got in. The band were going up into Canada some place from this little hick town and they hung around waiting for Joe but his plane was late. That stupid Frenchy, the road manager, wouldn't wait and so while I was sitting all by myself in that little airport, here comes Joe. "Where are the guys?" he says.

"They took off. They couldn't wait thirty minutes for you," I replied. Poor Joe. That was a hell of an introduction to a new band. He took another plane and eventually made the show that night and he stayed for around four years with them.

Sitting around my home in Los Angeles I used to read the music papers to see where the band was, from time to time. I was glad not to be out there with them, I know that. They had so many changes in the personnel during the ten years after I left, but Louis kept them together and they still packed them in. Through the years, whenever they would come out to California, I would go to see them, but mostly they were always traveling. I guess that's what finally wore Louis down: all that traveling. In 1969 he was seriously ill and a lot of people thought that he wouldn't make it, but, like the trooper he was, he got back in shape but was laid off blowing for a while. He could sing, but he wasn't supposed to play the horn: doctor's orders.

In 1970, for his seventieth birthday, they were planning a great big show here in Los Angeles and were planning to call it *Hello Louis!* It was originally the idea of a friend of mine, a jazz fan, named Floyd Levin. The actual show was put on by a group called "The Association of Southern California Jazz Clubs," and was held at the Shrine Auditorium. The promoters were afraid that they wouldn't have too many people there, but the thing came out like a gift. The place was packed and jammed.

Everybody wanted to play for Louis, to wish him happy birthday. Up to the last minute, Louis himself wasn't sure he could be there in person, because he was sick in bed. The day before the show he finally had permission to travel and so he arrived in LA.

They knew that he could play but he and Hoagy Carmichael did some mugging on the stage that night and they had a great big cake, several stories high on stage for him. Our group was called "Ambassador Satch" and Clark Terry played trumpet, Benny Carter and myself, reeds, Tyree Glenn, trombone, Joe Bushkin, piano, Red Callender, bass and Louis Bellson was the drummer. We had played our first number on the stage and I went into my feature number *C-Jam Blues* when Louis came rushing out from the wings and stopped the band dead. I wondered what the hell was going on. Apparently, somebody backstage had said that the show was running so late that someone would have to get Louis to cut down his act. Louis was in the wings behind a curtain, and overheard the remark. "No-one's going to cut down *my* act," he said and rushed on stage and stopped the band. I recall he went into *Hello Dolly* and several other big hits of his. It was really a great tribute to the man and I know he appreciated it deeply. It probably meant more to him than anything else. After all he was seventy and he had been near death a few months before.

The very last time I talked with Louis was on his seventy-first birthday. We had a little party at Floyd Levin's house and someone suggested that we call Louis and Lucille to wish him happy birthday. We all got on different phones and Lucille answered. We got to talking and Lucille said that Louis was resting. We said, "Don't disturb him. Let him rest." But Oh! He just had to talk. Lucille told us that she hadn't given him anything for his birthday yet and Louis said, "Pops. Lucille's gonna give me some of that Jelly-Roll for my birthday." And the poor guy's dying. Two days later he died in his sleep at his home in Corona.

TWENTY-THREE

"In the middle of a tour I read I had retired."

After I left Louis and the All Stars in 1961 I settled down to a life of gigging around Los Angeles. Sometimes guys would call and if I liked the deal I would go play. There were lots of jazz places I could have worked around the country if I had wanted to, but I was sick of the long hours that night club work entails. I had offers to take a band to New York or Chicago or other places, but I vowed that the days of working till two in the morning were over—for me at least. Let someone else do it if they wanted. Me, I just stayed around Los Angeles.

Lots of time I played with local bands. They had good musicians in the group but they had no musical organization. One time I was playing a gig and the bunch were stoned. I was playing the solo and all three of the horns were playing obbligato so loud behind me. I kept yelling, "Out, out," to make them stop, but they didn't hear nothing and so they went on the happy path. After that I gave up worrying so much and just took the things as they came. I worked with all kinds of guys: Dick Cary, Joe Darensbourg, Andrew Blakeney, George Orendorf. A whole bunch of them. To tell the truth, I really preferred the All Star kind of groups that promoters put together for a special show, a TV special or a jazz festival. You see here in LA if the people would realize what they have, they would appreciate it more, but it seems like they always wait for something big to happen. Say you're in Europe or something. When you come back here, then they'll recognize you where ordinarily they wouldn't. You're just an ordinary person. For instance, if I didn't have all the publicity, even in my home town, no one would pay any attention to me. They come up and say, "Don't you remember me. I went to school with you fifty years ago?" No, I don't know who they are and don't really care who they are, but you have to be nice to them. I don't pay no attention to those star-struck characters at all.

Good old Ben Pollack called me about playing for a month with him down in Palm Springs. He had a job at the El Mirador Hotel and it sounded like a good band. He had Warren Smith on trombone and Martin Pepe, trumpet, another good musician called Bernie something or other, I just can't recall his last name. Anyways, I took the job. That was the last time I played with Ben. He had lost the Pick-A-Rib place by then and he was working for his sister. At least she was backing him. Like I said the job lasted for a whole month and it felt good to be working every night again. Ben Pollack was such an easy-going guy to work for that you couldn't help but enjoy the music. In later years I was shocked when I read in the newspapers that Ben had hung himself down in Palm Springs. It was a terrible end to a nice guy.

The rest of the sixties I was mostly around here and had no plans to travel too much. I was happy, the way things were going, and I never had that "wanderlust" feeling some guys get. I think it was in 1970 that a guy called me from Colorado. His name was Dick Gibson and he was planning to start a series of Jazz Parties and had some of the top musicians in America attend. He put this proposition to me and it sounded good so I accepted. I went up there for four years straight and enjoyed every minute. He got around forty of the best guys possible and put together little sessions. You don't worry too much who you are playing with because they were all top men in the music profession. It's real great for the musicians because Dick is such a wonderful guy. He is the one that started the World's Greatest Jazz Band, by the way.

When I got up there to Vail, Colorado, they gave me a badge and wherever you go you just sign the tab and it's all taken care of. Your hotels are all paid for, your meals, your booze. They don't care about making a profit at all. I played with so many great men up at those parties: Milt Hinton, Vic Dickenson, Bobby Hackett, Tyree Glenn. Oh just so many.

Another guy that I liked to listen to and play with from those Dick Gibson things was Bob Wilber. He was a young guy and I knew him since he had been coming up. He was a disciple of Sidney Bechet and he plays a whole lot of soprano sax and clarinet. He doesn't just copy Sidney though. You can tell him from Bechet as he goes along because he plays a lot of original things. He can read like mad too and is quite a technician on the horn.

Like I said, those were great days at those Colorado parties. We really looked forward to them all year; to seeing our old friends. There was only a selected few people that got invited to attend and they paid a large sum per ticket but then they just went anywhere they wanted to without any admission. Jazz could use more things like that.

A little after the first of those Colorado affairs, I had a phone call from an old buddy, Art Hodes. Apart from playing real good piano, Art leads bands and arranges some tours. This time Columbia Artists Management had called him. One of their acts had canceled out and they were stuck. They send bands all over—bands, acts, plays—for like a season of shows and then the local promoters sell season tickets to all the shows at one go. Anyway, they called Art and asked him to put together a good jazz band and plug the hole left by this canceling act. Art called me and since I wasn't doing anything that I couldn't get away from, and since the tour was only for a few weeks and the money was good, I told him I'd go. He called the band "The Stars of Jazz," and we had Wild Bill Davison, trumpet, myself, Jim Beebe, trombone, Art at the piano and like master-of-ceremonies. Eddie Condon came with his guitar, Rail Wilson, bass, and Hillard Brown, drums.

Art got a real good one together with those guys. He used to introduce the men each night and it really wasn't hard work. Everyone was surprised the way the people ate up what we were doing. Every place we played the place was packed with older folks. They were the season ticket holders. Backstage at every place we worked they had a group of youngsters working all the lights and curtains. These youngsters had never heard music like this and they couldn't keep their feet still. Word must have gotten around because before you knew it the whole place was half and half, young and old.

They were some characters on that tour. Wild Bill Davison: all I can say is that they ought to write a book about him and his exploits. Poor Eddie Condon. That was his last trip. He died a while after. He was sick on that trip, but then he was always sick. He did all that drinking, all of his life, and there was something phenomenal about that guy. He could stay a week off that liquor then he would go right back on it. He was a funny guy. He never carried any cash on him during that whole tour. He always wrote checks. That was Eddie Condon. One time we were in a restaurant and all he had was a cup of coffee. His tab was 15 cents and he started to write a check, so the guy at the cashier's desk told him, "It's only 15 cents. What are you writing a check for?" Eddie'd say, "Take this or nothing." They really brought him along because so many people knew him for his contributions to jazz, his night club in New York, and his books that he wrote. He would sit there all night and play, but to be honest, I never heard a note he played. He seemed to play so quietly. Maybe he was good in his day, but during the Stars of Jazz tour I couldn't tell you what he played like because I never heard him. People loved him though because he was a character.

The tour started from New York. We had one rehearsal at Jimmy Ryan's little club off Broadway. We didn't really do anything but run down the solo pieces that each guy featured himself on. We only stayed there for around an hour. It was no problem as we all knew the tunes. After all they were just standard jazz numbers; no music to bother with. The only problem on that tour was that we had an "evil" bus driver. He was a pain in the neck. That was the only bad thing.

We went by bus everywhere. We went to Georgia, North Carolina, South Carolina, Mississippi and all over the South. The closest we ever got to New Orleans was Shreveport, Louisiana. Dottie came on the trip and she was the only wife there. Art's son and his daughter went along to help out. One time they bought a music paper and read me a passage where they were saying that I had retired from the music business. That was funny. I was in the middle of a tour when I read I had retired. Oh well!

Jim Beebe, our trombonist, was a nice guy. His father was a doctor and Jim came from Chicago. He was a friend of Hillard Brown, our drummer. They had been working with Art Hodes in Chicago with a trio just before they came on the trip. Hillard turned out to be a really good drummer and a nice time keeper. He had a grocery store back in Chicago and he told me that one year he made $250,000 from it. I never could figure out what he was doing out there with us playing music. Maybe he just wanted to get out of his store for a while.

After the tour broke up we all went home for the proverbial rest. I know the trip had been successful because the next year they wanted me to go again, but I couldn't make it on account of an offer I had to go to play at the New Orleans Jazz Festival. George Wein's office had called and asked if I would play the 1972 New Orleans Jazz Festival. Everything about the deal was OK and so I went. I had asked George Wein who would I be playing with and he told me that it would be a five-piece group. Wild Bill Davison, trumpet, himself on piano, me and "the best there is available in the City" on bass and drums. If the guys he got were the best, God alone knows what the worst sounded like. I mean these two guys were just be-bop cats and poor Bill and I could hardly think for listening to that junk they were laying down behind us. I gave George Wein holy hell for putting those characters with us. I mean the rhythm was lousy, just terrible. Naturally, the people applauded, but it could have been so good.

It had been twenty years since I had been back to New Orleans. I found it to be just as free and easy a town but the people were still the same as fifty years ago. One of the first guys I ran into was Louis Barbarin, the brother of Paul. Louis is also a drummer and quite good, so we talked a little about old times and I took a walk down to Felix's Restaurant near Canal Street. I practically lived there. I love oysters and they had the freshest and best you could ask for.

I just played the one concert down there but I stayed a whole week and so I got to get around some of the places. I went to where Wallace Davenport was working. There was nobody in there because they charged such ridiculous prices. I ordered a beer and got a "shorty" for $2.50. Wallace is a good trumpet player to listen to, but at those prices I'm not surprised the place was empty. Another night I went to the Preservation Hall, which is a joke. That's about the worst thing I've ever seen: dirtiest place and nothing exciting happening. The band I heard was Kid Thomas's Band. I don't know what he was doing. He played his trumpet into a derby, and he'd "wa-wa." Then he'd sit for another hour and "wa-wa" again. He wasn't playing nothing. Maybe I was expecting too much, because I had heard that he was supposed to be the nearest thing to Freddie Keppard. I don't know who the hell said that. Whoever it was never knew Freddie Keppard. Hell, no. Kid Thomas's tone was nothing like Keppard. Freddie could take a note and hold it, playing soft, and bring it out and shake up this whole building. I tell you Freddie Keppard was a *musician*.

I took a trip out to see my brother Alex one day. The poor guy was going deaf and couldn't work or play his drums. They still had him paying union dues, after all the years that he had been in that union. Out here in LA they would have made him an honorary member years ago, but that's New Orleans for you.

At the end of that week I had done my job and, apart from the oyster restaurant, I decided I didn't miss anything about New Orleans when I was leaving to come back to Los Angeles. I know one thing. People say how the music is still intact down there after seventy years. Shucks, if any of those bands that are in New Orleans today played at Tom Anderson's Cabaret, where Albert Nicholas and I worked in the early 1920's, the people would have run out.

TWENTY-FOUR

"Finally they sent a Rolls-Royce."

Over the last five years I had a few good offers and a load of bad offers. It's great to be able to pick your spots. The best feeling on earth. I get guys writing to me or calling me wanting me to do a tour here, a tour there. "Oh Mr Bigard," they say, "It won't be a hard tour." Well, I've got news for them. There ain't no such thing as an easy tour.

Most of my bookings come through personal friends inside the band booking business. If I go out on a tour it is generally for George Wein or Barry Martyn. Both of these guys are musicians and understand how it feels to be out on tour. I have worked many times with pick-up groups that George books or plays in and likewise I have done many guest spots with Barry Martyn's Legends of Jazz. We even made a nice record with the latter for Crescent Jazz Productions.

It was George, that booked me for the Newport Jazz Festival in NY, and three times in the last few years at the Nice Jazz Festival in France. I enjoyed the trips very much. Over the last few years I have made it a stipulation that if they want me, they have to take Dottie too. I see no reason why I would want to be out there in the boondocks, or the world's biggest cities for that matter, without my wife. I mostly go because I feel like it. I had been careful to put that money aside, all my life, for my September years. Of course I still get royalty checks for my compositions and so I can always get by if the phone never rings.

When George Wein asked me about Nice, I wanted to go. I have always loved France, and I can always get me a brand-new beret while I'm there. The first time I went it was great, just sitting out in the sun on the French Riviera. They had all kinds of good musicians there, and we played almost the same kind of pattern as in the Colorado Jazz Parties. Jam-session stuff, but with first-class musicians. They had a couple of New Orleans bands over there including a brass band, but it wasn't too much. There was a big husky guy that seemed to be leading it. He played all in eighth notes or sixteenths, but all out of tune. I'll never know what ears some guys have that they can't hear when they're out of tune.

That tour actually started when we left New York. Dotty and I flew over to Rome with Eddie "Cleanhead" Vinson and his wife. Cozy Cole, Arvell and Milt Buckner came on the same plane too, I seem to recall. When we got to Rome they met us with a bus and we had to ride a further six hours to get to where we were going to play. It was a town called Pescara, down on the eastern side of the Italian "boot." We played there one night, then back on that bus to Rome and flew right into Nice. I played with everybody there, and heard so much jazz. They had just so much going on that even the customers couldn't catch everything that was happening. It was great, but I was glad to get back home.

When I got back my two friends Barry Martyn and Floyd Levin had formed a company and were calling it "Crescent Jazz Productions." They were planning to open a show in Los Angeles and call it "A Night in New Orleans." They were going to get together some of the best traditional jazz talent in the country and hoped that it would catch on and become a yearly thing. They even talked about expanding the show and taking it to Europe and all over the USA. They asked me to headline it, and I said that I would. When the show opened that first night it was sold right out. You couldn't buy a seat, and, in fact, they had to sell space that they never ever sold, behind pillars in the theater.

It was a great idea—one of the best that I've heard of in quite some time—and it was put on right. Of course there were some weak spots, but it can't all be perfect. Over the next few years they did take the show to Europe. Three times in fact. We played some of the biggest concert halls. At the Stadthalle in Vienna, Austria, we drew some eight thousand people and we sold out the Berlin Philharmonic twice. Every other year the show went to Europe and each September it played Los Angeles. One of the most memorable sessions I ever played on that show was with my old Ellingtonian trumpet-playing friend Ray Nance. He came out specially from New York just to do the one show. He didn't know it but he was dying. He was on this dialysis treatment.

Ray played trumpet and violin, I played clarinet, Duke Burrell, piano, Bobby Stone, bass and Louis Bellson, drums. It was like a salute to Duke Ellington but we played some unusual stuff. I remember we played *Poor Butterfly*, a beautiful number. The thing that knocked everybody out was Ray Nance playing *Come Sunday* on his violin. So beautiful.

Another year they expanded the show to three nights and called it the *Los Angeles Jazz Festival*. There was one night of blues music, one night that Joe Venuti headed and the third night I played in a show called *Memories of Satchmo*. Teddy Buckner played Louis, and they also had most of the original band: Trummy Young, Cozy Cole, Dick Cary and Red Callender. It was kicks to be back with the old gang once more.

Sometime in the last few years I made one solo tour with a really nice bunch of guys from Switzerland called the "New Ragtime Orchestra." They were led by a clarinet man named Jacky Milliet. Dottie and I had a really happy time playing with them, and they treated us like we were royalty. It was really fun. I hadn't done a solo tour outside of the US before. Not to play all by myself that is. I didn't regret taking that trip.

Sometime around 1975 I formed a trio called "The Pelican Trio" with Duke Burrell, piano and Barry Martyn, drums. This was the first time that I had played in so small a group, for I can't remember how long. We made some appearances around Los Angeles at a place called the Mayfair Music Hall in Santa Monica, and we also made a record. That record was a pleasure. We each picked a couple of songs and each one of us arranged how our choice would go. It was more of a co-operative ideas group than any band I had worked with. We rehearsed once a week for a long while, and in fact still do rehearse just before we have anything coming up.

We went on the road with the trio the first time in 1978 with *A Night in New Orleans*, the package show. We played Vancouver, Anchorage, Alaska, Edmonton then jumped over to open the next night in Düsseldorf, Germany. While we were in Europe we played Torino, Italy, Frankfurt, Zurich and a lot of other capitals. We had about twenty-three people traveling in a great long bus like a greyhound. It had a bar in the back with an ice-box. The driver always kept the ice-box filled with cold beers and some little bottles of liquor. After the show wound up we played one date with the trio in London before we came back home. It was a tiring tour, but I was glad that the trio went over so well.

After being a musician for nearly sixty years you have a number of ambitions that over the years you somehow manage to fulfil. Like playing Carnegie Hall, for instance. Well I did that. Several times. My other kick happened on one of the *Night In New Orleans* tours. We were playing at the Royalty Theatre in London and we got off the plane at London Airport. They had two or three buses to meet us all but I heard a guy paging Mr Barney Bigard and Mr Barry Martyn. Here comes a little guy with a beard. "I've been sent to pick you up," he says. It turned out that his boss was a fan of ours and owned a big car-sales place in the country somewhere. His name was Martin Colvill. His business was selling or renting sports cars or luxury cars to people. He was away in France and couldn't make our concert but he sent his chauffeur—this little bearded guy, Stevie—out to the airport to meet us. "Mr Colvill says that I am to take you anywhere you want to go in London while you are here," says Stevie.

We stood by the baggage claim while he went to get the car. Up he came with this real beautiful Jaguar. I mean this thing was a beaut. We got in and he drove us to the hotel and like he said, "anywhere we wanted to go." On the way I was just kidding and I said, "You would have thought that they would at least have sent a Rolls." This little Stevie must have picked up on that because when we were in the hotel lobby that night, waiting for him to get us to go to the concert, here he comes. "She's outside," says Stevie.

When we got out to the sidewalk I couldn't believe it. Here was a brand-new great big black, shiny Rolls-Royce. It had a bar, telephone and a sliding electric window between us and Stevie. We rode to London in style that night. As I was sitting there crossing over the downtown suburbs all dark and brick, I thought back to my early days in New Orleans when I would gather brick dust to make a few nickels for the show, to my teacher Lorenzo Tio, to my days with King Oliver, Duke Ellington, Louis Armstrong and so many others. It seemed far away and long ago that night, as we drove to work in London.

Finally, after fifty years, they sent a Rolls-Royce.

Index

Turtle Twist, 60
Twelfth Street Rag, 102

Vail, Colorado, 138
Vallee, Rudy, 51
Vancouver, 144
Venuti, Joe, 144
Victor (record company), 59, 60
Vienna: Stadthalle, 143
Vigne, Sidney, 16–17
Vinson, Eddie "Cleanhead", 143
——wife, 143
Virginia Beach, 76
Vista, nr Oceanside, California, 125, 127
Vodery, Will, 64

Waller, Fats, 45
Ward, Ada, 58
Waring, Fred: Fred Waring and his Pennsylvanians
 (band), 132
Warneke, Louis, 37
Warren, Earle, 72
Washington DC, 46, 101
Watson, Leo, 81
Watters, Lu, 89
——, Yerba Buena Jazz Band (with Turk Murphy),
 89
Webb, Chick, 53, 60–1
——, band, 53
Webster, Ben, 54, 73, 78
Wein, George, 140, 142
Weintraub, Charlie, 131
Welk, Lawrence, 102
Welles, Orson, 85–6

West, Mae, 60
Whaley, Wade, 85
Where the Blues was Born in New Orleans, 93
Whetsol, Artie, 55, 56–7, 64, v, vii
White, Amos, 12, 13
——, band, 21
White, Harry, 55
White, Johnny, 130
Whiting, Margaret, 84
Who's Sorry Now, 64
Wilber, Bob, 138
Wild Cat Blues, 71
Williams, Clarence, 60, 71
Williams, Cootie, 22, 52, 53, 55, 67, v, vii
Williams, Mary Lou, 73
Willow Weep for Me, 54
Wilson, Buster, 85, 86, ix
Wilson, Rail, 139
Wilson, Teddy, 77
Wilson, Udell, 24
World War II, 75
Wyoming, 76

Yancey, Jimmy, 83
Young, Lester, 72, 73
Young, Robert, 89
Young, Trummy, 103, 121–2, 132, 133, 134, 144,
 xiv, xv
Ysaguirre, Bob, 21
Yukl, Joe, 123, xv

Zeno, Henry, 10
Ziegfeld, Flo, 49
Zurich, 144